ANNIE'S ATTIC MYSTERIES™

Boxed In

Karen Kelly

AnniesMysteries.com

Boxed In

Library of Congress-in-Publication Data
Boxed In / by Karen Kelly
p. cm.
ISBN: 978-1-59635-380-0
I. Title
2011900303

AnniesMysteries.com
800-282-6643
Annie's Attic Mysteries™
Series Creator: Stenhouse & Associates, Ridgefield, Connecticut
Series Editors: Ken and Janice Tate

10 11 12 13 14 | Printed in China | 10 9 8 7 6 5 4 3 2 1

1

"Boots, you sentimental old cat, there's no reason for you to be cranky with me. I was only gone a week." Annie Dawson bent down to scratch the gray cat under her chin. Boots closed her eyes, stretching her chin forward to get a better angle for enjoyment. "All forgiven?"

As if coming to her senses, Boots's eyes popped back open and she turned away from Annie. She sidestepped away from the legs of her human housemate without rubbing against them as usual. Apparently, forgiveness was going to be a process. Boots had been even more eccentric than usual since Annie's friend and neighbor had brought the cat back home. "I know Alice spoiled you rotten while I was in Texas, so don't try to make me feel guilty." Boots's tail jerked quickly forward before she padded down the hall from the kitchen to the living room, jumped onto the couch and settled down among the pillows.

Annie picked up her Lone Star coffee mug to take a final sip. Concerns had lurked in Annie's mind before the trip to celebrate her twin grandchildren's birthdays. Would she find it too hard to leave her daughter, son-in-law, grandchildren, and friends again to return to Stony Point, Maine? Would staying in the home she had shared so many years with her late husband, Wayne, bring fresh grief? Would she regret her decision to allow her church in Texas to use her home as a missionary retreat? But, like the cup of French roast coffee she'd just finished, the trip had satisfied and invigorated her.

Annie washed out her mug at the sink, setting it on the drain board to dry. As she walked down the hall to grab her purse and a sweater, the doorbell rang. *That's got to be Alice*, she thought. Before she could get close enough to reach out for the doorknob, a gray blur shot out from the living room. Boots planted herself, her back to the door with her fur fluffed, a miniature dragon protecting her treasure. "Boots, don't be silly." Annie stepped closer and reached to open the door. The cat put up a paw to bat at her trouser-covered legs. "Hey, watch those claws."

From the other side of the door came Alice's voice. "Annie, is that you? What's up with the door—another chore for Wally?"

"I'm being held hostage by an ornery feline! I wonder if Wally does hostage negotiation." Annie laughed as she bent down to try and scoot Boots out of the path of the door. The cat simply sidestepped along the door, and Annie scooted only air. The door remained blocked.

"Try a Kitty Crunchies bribe. If that doesn't work, call her bluff and open the door anyway. Boots won't let herself get whacked with this old heavy door. Cats are creatures of self-preservation." Alice's voice lilted with semi-suppressed giggles.

"That's why she stays. She knows a softie when she sees one." Annie turned her back on the topic of the conversation, heading back to the kitchen. Pulling out the box of Kitty Crunchies from a bottom cabinet, she shook the box as she walked slowly back. She put on what she thought of as her best bribe voice, crooning, "What does a dragon kitty need to turn back into a beautiful Boots? Come get some Kitty Crunchies." Looking back at the door as though weighing her options, Boots straightened her tail into the air and abandoned her post. Annie poured a good portion into Boots's bowl and gave her a quick pat before rescuing Alice from the porch.

"How long is she going to give me this treatment? Will we go through this every time I go on a trip?" Annie said as Alice entered the foyer.

"I think she'll snap out of it pretty fast. But don't rely on the Kitty Crunchies too often, or she may decide to make it permanent." Alice shuddered but couldn't hide her grin.

"Good point. I also don't want to quadruple my budget for cat treats. Hey, I need to go to town this morning to find Wally. Do you know where he's working this week?"

"At Ian's house, I think. I heard him mention it to Peggy this weekend at The Cup & Saucer. I was planning to go to town too. Want to ride together? I'll put the top down." Alice took the keys to her Mustang convertible from her jeans pocket and dangled them in front of Annie.

"Second successful bribe of the day, and it's not even nine o'clock yet! Use your powers for good, friend." Annie scooped up her purse and sweater from the hallway table. She lowered her voice. "We better slip out fast."

Alice cocked an ear toward the kitchen. The soft sound of crunching seemed to be slowing. She opened her eyes wide in mock terror and tiptoed to the door. Turning the knob, she opened it inch by inch to keep it from creaking. They kept their silence until safely in the convertible. Alice slowly backed out of the driveway onto Ocean Drive.

"Did you find more repairs at Grey Gables for Wally?" Alice asked. "Don't tell me something broke while you were gone."

"I do have some work for him, but no repairs this time." Annie tied an oversized red scarf under her hair and tucked away the stray layers of blond hair so she wouldn't have to fight tangles when they arrived in town. "The toy lobster boat Wally made for John's birthday was a huge hit at the twins' birthday party. I have quite a list of Brookfield mothers who can't wait for Wally to make one for each of their own children."

"Oh, Peggy will be so thrilled! This will be one year Wally and Peggy won't have to struggle for income in the winter season. Emily might be able to keep her dancing lessons for the whole year. Annie, what a blessing." Alice put her right hand up for a high five.

Meeting the raised hand with her own, Annie responded, "I hope this will give Wally the encouragement to realize that he does have the ability to support his family. He has thought of himself as a borderline failure for too long." Though he had developed into an excellent handyman, depended upon by the Stony Point homeowners to keep their homes and businesses in sound working order, Wally had had trouble putting the memories of his troubled youth away for good. "I can't wait to see his face when he sees the orders."

"If it wouldn't freak him out, I'd love to get a photo of his reaction." Alice rounded a curve and switched on her turn signal at Maple Street. Mornings in late summer were fresh and crisp, reminders that ripe apples of the same nature would be filling the orchards soon.

"Ah, the lupines are sprouting." Annie nodded to the right where the sandy and rock-dotted soil on the roadside made the perfect nursery for the hardy plants. "I always loved the Texas bluebonnets back home. Here I get to enjoy even more colors—purple, pink, blue—they're just glorious. Looks like we'll have plenty to enjoy next summer."

"Just don't get any ideas about transplanting them for your garden." Alice shook a finger, setting a bangle bracelet dancing, "Remember."

"Been trying not to, thank you very much," Annie said with a sheepish grin. "I was twelve. How was I supposed to know lupines are aphid magnets."

"Good thing for you Betsy was good-natured and believed in learning from mistakes," Alice said, referring to Annie's grandmother, Betsy Holden, who had passed away the previous year, leaving her rambling oceanside home to Annie. "But I didn't enjoy spending those summer hours in Betsy's garden conducting a search-and-destroy mission instead of beachcombing."

"I can hear her now. 'If Thomas Edison had stopped at his first hundred mistakes, we'd still be using tallow candles and oil lamps.'" Annie's smile shaded with wistfulness. "I hope I never forget her voice. Or Wayne's."

"Some people are better at remembrance than others. Like Betsy, you're a memory keeper." Alice turned into a long driveway, leading to the Butler house. Like many of the houses on the outskirts of Stony Point, it was well over a hundred years old. And unlike the town, which had had to be rebuilt three times due to its history of battles, it had aged gracefully with help from a great deal of elbow grease supplied by the Butler family. "There's Wally's truck. I guess my memory isn't so bad, either. Short-term, anyway."

Annie slid off her scarf and tucked it into a side pocket of her purse. As she and Alice climbed out of the Mustang, the door of the Butler house opened. Ian Butler filled the doorway with his almost military posture and ever-present energy.

"Alice and Annie, good morning! To what do I owe this pleasure?" During her time in Stony Point Annie had seen Mayor Ian Butler excited, perplexed, frustrated, determined, pleased, and almost every other emotion in existence. What she had never seen him was bored. Today was no exception. Ian was always carpe diem personified.

"Ian, I'm sorry to just drop by like this. I thought you'd already be in town, plunging into your mayoral duties," Annie answered.

"It's true I'm leaving a little later than on a typical day. Wally and I are strategizing our plan of attack on aging bathrooms." Ian's look of glee gave the two women a glimpse of what the mayor of Stony Point looked like at ten years old.

"It's Wally I actually came to talk with. But don't worry, I'm not going to try to wrangle him away from you before he's brought your bathrooms into submission."

"That's probably the easiest request I'll hear all day. Wally's in the downstairs bathroom today. Down the center hall, second door on the left." Ian held the door open for them until they stepped into the foyer. "I'll be in the study, if you need me," Ian pointed to the French doors across from the living room.

Industrious sounds coming from down the hall made

Ian's directions to Wally unnecessary. "Hi, Wally. How's the bathroom coming?" Annie raised her voice over the sounds of tile removal. Wally was standing in a rubble of tile chunks with hammer in one hand and putty knife in the other. Chink, chink. Another bit of tile tumbled to the floor. Wally turned around, set the knife down on the corner of the sink, and then pushed his safety glasses up with the back of his hand.

"Ayuh, Annie. Alice. Watch your step. Broken tile can cut through shoe soles." Porcelain dust aged Wally's thick head of hair. "Did you have a good time in Texas?"

"It was a wonderful week. I've never seen John as excited with a gift as he was with the toy boat you made."

"That's real good to hear, Annie. Emily's been helping me make her ballerina boat. Course, it's nothing like anything you'll ever see chugging into Stony Point harbor." The three chuckled at the thought.

"How long do you think it will take for you to finish with Emily's boat? The reason I ask is ..." Annie reached into her purse and took out a piece of paper. She offered it to Wally. "John wasn't the only one who loved his boat. This is a list of mothers who are hoping you will be able to make boats for their children too. Your lobster boat is a hit."

Wally's mouth opened, and he drew in a surprised breath as he saw the list of names and contact information. Annie leaned over and pointed to a number she'd written at the top.

"That's the price they'd like to pay. Is that all right?"

"All right? I thought what you paid me was too much! Are they sure?" Wally blinked his eyes several times. His hands were too dusty to rub his eyes, so he blinked instead, as though he expected the numbers to rearrange themselves with each blink.

"The ladies were very sure. Toy or specialty stores would probably charge even more for boats with inferior construction. So many companies are selling disposable, low-quality toys these days that people appreciate your boat because it will last to be handed down for generations to come."

"Annie's right, Wally," Alice chimed in. "The toys we had when we were growing up didn't break very easily. That's why we still find them in Betsy's attic. It's hard to find toys that will last now."

Wally was mentally adding up the profit for each boat. Excitement built with each addition. "This will make up for my usual winter shortfall. Emily can dance through the winter! Might even be able to put some aside."

"Make sure you tell me when the Christmas recital is," Annie said.

Alice chimed in, "Me too."

"I will, I will." Puffs of dust floated into the air with Wally's enthusiastic nod.

"We don't want to keep you from your tile, so we'll head out now. We both have errands in town," said Alice.

"If you see Peggy, would you please not tell her about the boat orders? I want to surprise her tonight." Wally realized he was not giving them an easy task. His wife could coax information from the tightest lips.

"We promise to do our best, but you know Peggy. Good thing the KGB never had someone like her on their side. The Cold War might have been very different," Alice quipped.

"You're telling me. Try hiding an anniversary present

from her." Wally's shy grin spread again across his face as he folded and tucked the order list into a pocket in his carpenter pants.

Annie and Alice left Wally to his hammer and knife. "That was a fun way to start the day," Annie said. "I feel a little like a fairy godmother."

"We'll pick you up a wand at Malone's Hardware while we're in town. Mike carries a little of everything. He might even have some jars of fairy dust." Alice had just finished speaking when the door to the study opened. Ian popped his head into the hall.

"Did I hear someone say 'in town'? Would you ladies be interested in sharing a booth at The Cup & Saucer? I haven't had breakfast or coffee yet."

"Now that you mention it," said Annie, " I fed Boots but not myself."

"Last one there leaves the tip!" Alice laid down the gauntlet while scooting to the door. "Tie your scarf tight, Annie. We've got this one in the bag."

"We'll see about that!" The mayor grabbed his briefcase, and the race was on.

2

Annie and Alice tumbled through the door of The Cup & Saucer, breathless from laughter. Peggy came toward them with platters of pancakes and eggs lined along her arms.

"Has a nor'easter blown into harbor?" she asked.

Annie pushed her scarf off her head, her eyes scanning the booths. "We're having a little race with the mayor. And it looks like we've won!"

"I knew it was a sure thing." Alice's eyes twinkled as her words came out in quick little bursts. "A Mustang will beat any car driven by a mayor with a reputation to protect."

Annie glanced out the window. "He's coming down the street. Quick! There's a booth." Peggy laughed as she took the food she was holding to a table of hungry sightseers. Annie and Alice slid into the left seat of the booth just as Ian entered the diner. The women simultaneously waved, waggling their fingers playfully.

Ian strode over to the booth. He stopped about a foot from the table and dropped down into a deep bow. "M'ladies, you have vanquished this humble public servant."

"Have no fear, Sir Butler," said Alice. "You will live to race, and lose, another day."

"Be careful you don't underestimate the mayor's competitive spirit," replied Annie, "or gumption, as we call it in Texas."

Ian remained in his bow.

"It's going to be difficult to drink coffee in that position," Alice teased. "And Peggy's coming." Ian straightened and took his seat opposite the two women. Peggy filled the space he had vacated, setting a mug in front of each of them and pouring coffee.

"Annie, out with it now. How did John like the lobster boat?" Her blue eyes stared into Annie's green ones as she tapped out a rhythm on the table with her free hand. Tiny lobsters had replaced the tiny flags that had decorated her nails in July. Peggy's beautician sister, Mitzy, had outdone herself this month.

Annie resisted the urge to nudge Alice with her elbow. "LeeAnn could hardly drag John and his friends away from the boat—even for his very favorite birthday cake and cookies and cream ice cream! I was worried for a minute he would try to float it in the punch bowl and lay out the traps."

"I told Wally that boat was a beauty, but he kept worrying about whether he had made it right or not." Pride radiated from Peggy's blue eyes. "Now, do you three want your usuals or are you going to change things up?"

"Apparently, I'm the only one who actually ate breakfast this morning. Coffee's all I need," answered Alice.

Annie reached over to check the menu sheet. Peggy nodded at Ian. "Mayor?"

"I got creative last week so I'll have the usual."

"If by creative you mean having rye toast instead of wheat, I guess that's true." Peggy winked at the two women and turned to Annie.

"Well, I'm going to need lots of energy today. I'll have

oatmeal with walnuts and raisins." Annie raised her coffee mug to her lips. "What?" she asked as three pairs of expectant eyes settled on her.

"Energy for … another mystery?" Ian guessed.

"Definitely not! I have much too much to do without that. Uh, Peggy, I think Jeff is trying to get your attention." Annie pointed her spoon toward the counter, where the owner was waving a spatula.

"Oh, blast! Fill me in when your food is ready." Peggy bustled across the room to hang the two orders on the wheel and then refill coffee mugs at the tables.

Alice nudged Annie. "Go on."

"Spending the week with LeeAnn and the twins was such a joy. As I told Peggy, John was so excited about his lobster boat and Joanna loved her doll and the matching sweaters, but most of all, we all enjoyed each other so much that—"

"You're not moving back to Texas, are you?" Alice interrupted. "I know it sounds selfish, but I found my best friend after so long. It would be hard to see you go again." Ian stayed silent, his intense gaze focused on the sugar dispenser.

Annie smiled. "What I was going to say is that I talked to LeeAnn again about the family coming to Stony Point for a visit. I think she's warming to the idea."

"Awesome! I'm so relieved," Alice stirred her coffee a little too enthusiastically. Thin brown rivulets trickled down the side of the mug. "Of course, I've been wanting to meet your daughter and the twins. I feel like I already know them."

"I'm thinking if I can put together some ideas of day trips and fun things to do, LeeAnn's 'maybe' will grow up to a 'definite.' And of course, I want to have Grey Gables ready for their visit. There's still much to be done to make it safe for the twins to explore."

"I'll help with Grey Gables," Alice volunteered, "if Boots will let me in."

The whirlwind that was Peggy set food in front of Annie and Ian. "So what did I miss?"

"Plans for a visit from Annie's daughter and grandkids," answered Alice.

"That sounds like so much fun. Do you think your granddaughter would like to meet Emily?" Peggy spoke at top speed before her boss could notice her lingering.

"I think they could be great friends." Annie smiled. "Though I hope they don't get into as much mischief as Alice and I did on my visits!"

"What's life without a little mischief?" Peggy asked before she whirled on to another booth.

"Annie, I'd be glad to help you with ideas for ways your family can enjoy our town and state." No longer contemplating the sugar, Ian's smile had returned. "How about a whale-watch tour on a real lobster boat? Do you know when they are most likely to visit?"

"John would flip, Ian! The twins are starting school this fall. That would make Thanksgiving break the most likely time for a visit." Annie sprinkled a little cinnamon onto her oatmeal and took a bite.

"Hmmmm, whale-watch season goes until the end of October. By Thanksgiving, it's pretty miserable out there." Ian paused for a moment. "But I bet the Maine Maritime Museum would capture his imagination."

"Oh, that sounds perfect. Where is it?" Annie set down her

spoon to pull a small notebook and a pen out of her purse.

"In Bath, just one county over. It would be an easy day trip with plenty of time to enjoy the town," Ian answered. "I'm surprised you and Alice haven't been there yet."

"Hey, I *do* have to work occasionally," Alice defended herself.

"Yes, you do," said Ian. "Your Princessa and Divine Décor businesses help keep our town a charming place to live and visit."

"I'll have to make sure it's open Thanksgiving week," Annie said as she wrote down the name and location of the museum.

"It's only closed on Thanksgiving Day, and all of you will be in town that day for the Stony Point Community Thanksgiving Dessert, won't you?" asked Ian.

"Your grandkids will go nuts over all the dessert choices," said Alice. "Most families feast in early afternoon to make sure they can sample several by seven p.m." She picked up her coffee mug and took a sip.

"I have some brochures from the Maritime Museum at the office. Come by and pick one up before you and Alice leave town." Ian took the final bite of his toast. "I'd better get to the office, as pleasant as this start to my day has been."

Alice winked at Annie. "Mr. Mayor, don't forget to give Peggy a *nice* tip."

"I always pay my debts," Ian grinned as he slid out of the booth. "Ladies." He gave another bow, shorter this time, and went to the register to pay his bill. As he walked past them on his way to the door, Alice and Annie gave him the same wave they had when he had first walked in.

"That was fun," Annie said before taking another spoonful of her oatmeal.

"You know, Ian seemed a little out of sorts while you were in Texas." Alice moved over to the empty side of the booth.

"You have an overactive imagination, Alice," Annie said. "I'm sure he wasn't any different at all."

"Actually, Alice is telling the truth," Peggy announced as she topped off the remaining coffee mugs and picked up Ian's mostly empty plate. "I didn't think he'd ever get over Arianna when she died. But now …"

"You two are starting to scare me." Annie pushed the last dollops of oatmeal around the bowl. "I spent the past week in the home I shared with Wayne for more than two decades. The thought of giving my heart to any man again makes me numb—terror-numb."

For once Peggy only nodded. Alice reached across the table to pat Annie's hand.

"I appreciate Ian's friendship, and I know I can rely on him if I need help. But that's as far as my feelings go, and I plan to keep it that way." Annie slid her bowl toward Peggy. "We better start on our errands, Alice. Peggy, what do we owe?"

"Nothing. Your friend paid the whole bill." Peggy grinned.

"If he's trying to soften me up for our next race, it won't work." Alice tossed her auburn hair behind her shoulders. "But I might just vote to re-elect him. See you at the meeting tomorrow, Peggy."

"If I can get away, you know you will." Peggy, a quilter, tried to take her morning break at the diner so that it coincided with Hook and Needle Club meetings each Tuesday at

A Stitch In Time, the local needlecraft shop.

Annie said good-bye, and the two friends left The Cup & Saucer.

"I need to pick up some organizing supplies from Malone's. How about you?" Annie asked, draping her sweater over her shoulders.

"Weather stripping for me. The carriage house is long on charm but short on insulation. I'm determined to have a warmer winter this year!" Alice hooked her arm through Annie's. "Malone's Hardware it is."

As they approached A Stitch in Time the door swung out, and Mary Beth Brock's head appeared. She motioned to the two women.

"Annie, are you enjoying our version of late summer after being in Texas?" the owner of Annie's favorite store asked.

"Mary Beth, 'enjoy' doesn't begin to capture it." Annie drew in a deep breath of the fresh coolness of the morning. "I loved my time in Texas, but I don't miss the heat and humidity!"

"I'm glad to have you back. We need your creativity for our next project. Yours too, Alice." Mary Beth never went long without cooking up a project or two. "The Harvest on the Harbor celebration is approaching fast. I want both of you to be thinking of ideas for the Hook and Needle Club theme this year. We want to raise plenty of money for the Thanksgiving Turkey Giveaway this year."

"So we know the why, just need the what?" Alice quipped.

"Exactly. We'll all share our ideas at tomorrow's meeting, and the group will select their favorite. Then we'll all get to work!" Mary Beth squinted and tilted her head toward somewhere behind Annie's right elbow. "Not even noon and already handprints! See you tomorrow!" Before the door closed all the way behind her, Annie and Alice heard Mary Beth call out to Kate Stevens, her assistant at the store. "Kate! Where's the vinegar spray?"

"I don't know how I will be able to concentrate enough to think of any themes," Annie confessed as they crossed Main Street to Malone's Hardware. "My mind is set on November. When is the Harvest on the Harbor?"

"Last week in September, as it is every year," answered Alice. "The town needs all the socializing it can get before winter turns us all into hibernating critters."

"And dentists gain more customers through caramel- and candy-apple mishaps."

"It's all in the biting technique. I'd be glad to teach it to you." Alice pushed open the door of Malone's Hardware.

"Gram never lost a tooth as far as I know. I'd like to keep the tradition going, so thanks for your offer. Now ... where's the organization section?"

Mike Malone called to them from behind the front counter. "Good morning, Annie and Alice. May I help you with anything today?"

"Point me to your weather stripping, Mike. My windows and doors failed the candle test in spectacular fashion. I want my cozy carriage house to actually *be* cozy this winter." Alice had learned many things through her failed marriage to John MacFarlane, but home improvement wasn't one of them. After pouring time into restoring her heart, now was the time to begin the restoration of her home.

"You have some options, Alice. Come with me to aisle three. Annie, I'll be with you in a minute."

"Oh, no need, Mike. I found the aisle for me." Annie moved her gaze from top to bottom of the nearly ceiling-high shelves that held the organizational products. Then she took a step to the right and repeated her visual scan. As she took in the different storage options, mental images of the kinds of clutter in the attic, library and bedrooms paraded in her mind's eye. She scribbled sizes, shapes and materials in the notebook she always carried tucked inside her purse. She was pleased by the variety of choices. Grey Gables obviously wasn't the only storage-challenged home in town. She was debating the merits of magazine holders versus file boxes for her grandfather's journals, when something round and hard pressed into her back.

"Don't move or ..." whispered a husky voice, "... or I'll *caulk* you!" Annie spun around just in time to witness Alice's attempt at twirling the caulk gun.

"Are you suggesting I'm leaking hot air?" For the second time that morning the two women collapsed against each other in giggles. Mike gently took the caulk gun from Alice and carried it to the counter with the amused look of one who, after raising five children, was more than used to shenanigans.

"Alice, we have caulk and gun and foam sealant for the exterior, and weather stripping for the interior windows and doors. That should make a significant difference in the cold season." Mike rang up the items.

Alice wiped the corners of her eyes. "Thanks, Mike, for your help."

Annie stacked two of the file boxes onto the counter and went back for a couple of see-through and stackable storage containers. "This will get me started. I'm sure I'll be back several times between now and Thanksgiving."

"Getting ready for your family's visit, eh?" Mike asked. The speed of information dissemination no longer startled Annie as it used to. She simply smiled as Mike added, "Is there anything else I can do for you?"

"Say hello to Fiona for us." Annie picked up her tall stack of storage stuff, while Alice slung her bag over her shoulder and fished in her pocket for her keys.

"I certainly will." Mike held the door open.

As the Mustang wound along Ocean Drive, Annie tilted her head back and closed her eyes, reveling in the play of warm sunshine and cool ocean air against her cheek. "On days like this, do you feel like you can accomplish anything?"

"I'm usually conflicted. Part of me is energized to tackle something … like weatherproofing." Alice broke into the tune of *I Am Woman* with slightly different lyrics. "I am woman, see me caulk! The wind can no more … mock or … stalk!"

Annie's humming along turned to groaning.

"OK, so I promise to never show up on *America's Got Talent*. But as I was saying earlier today, the other part of me wants to spend the day outside puttering in the garden or collecting sea glass on the beach."

"Sea glass! We haven't done that in ages." Annie made a mental note to add that to her list of things to do with Joanna and John. "I wonder how many pounds of sea glass you and I collected over my summer vacations."

"Why don't we have a conflict-free day and do both?" Alice pulled the Mustang over to the roomy shoulder of the road. They had come to a popular place for beachcombers to access the small sandy beach north of town. “It would be a shame for you to spend the rest of the day cooped up inside Grey Gables, as wonderful a place as it is.”

“Hmmm, that depends. Just how much help are you going to give me with getting the house ready for LeeAnn and the twins?”

“More than enough to earn a little sea-glass hunt.”

Annie was out of the car before Alice finished her sentence. Before disappearing through the break in the beach roses that lined the road, she tossed over her shoulder, “What’s taking you so long?”

3

Annie resembled an ostrich, her head disappearing into the back of her grandmother's antique corner cabinet. The beachcombing she had done the day before with Alice had netted a small but beautiful collection of white, green, amber and blue glass, and Annie knew just the dish to use to display them. Annie selected the small cut-glass sweetmeat dish and carefully lifted it from the cabinet. She shut the door and dropped the tiny latch over the knob. Footsteps sounded on the porch.

Annie set the dish on the rococo table and then glanced around for Boots as she strode to welcome Alice. Alice was putting her right hand up to the doorbell when Annie opened the door. "You beat Boots to the door! It must be a light-on-your-feet kind of day."

"I had a head start," Annie confessed. "I was in the living room, and Boots is upstairs, I think." Her eyes went to the basket hanging from Alice's left arm. "You brought your magical bread basket!"

"It doubles as a magical cookie basket too." Alice lifted the red and blue plaid cloth. "Molasses crinkles, to be exact."

Annie bent close to the basket and inhaled. "Ooooooh, heavenly! It's a good thing I already put on the coffee. I wouldn't have the strength to wait for brewing." As the two friends walked past the staircase, Boots, who had come to investigate the newcomer, stuck her face between two posts of the banister.

Alice laughed. "Boots is acting casual, but you know it's bugging her that I got in before she knew it."

"Good thing you did too. Too many Kitty Crunchies a fat kitty makes." In the kitchen Annie poured the coffee while Alice set the cookies on the kitchen table.

"How long did your energy last for your organizing yesterday?" Alice asked.

"Long enough to make a to-do list that would be considered big even in Texas." Annie selected a cookie and dipped it into her coffee. "I'm pretty sure I'm going to clean out Mike's entire aisle of storage options."

"You won't turn Betsy's attic into a complete plastic palace, though, will you?" Alice nibbled along the edge of her molasses crinkle.

"Absolutely not. Somehow I feel like I'd be dishonoring the spirit of Grey Gables if I did that." Part of the cookie in Annie's hand was showing signs of making an imminent plunge into her coffee. Annie bent her head and rescued it just in time. "Mercy! This is the best cookie I've ever tasted! I didn't think anything without chocolate could be so amazing."

"It's an old recipe from my family. Maybe I'll make them for the Thanksgiving Dessert."

"Then I'll come for sure. How's the weatherproofing coming along?" Annie asked as she snagged another cookie.

"I had a demonstration last night that I had to prepare for, so I didn't break out the caulk gun. But I will this afternoon. Cracks and gaps, beware!" Alice glanced at her Princessa watch, a gift from the company in recognition of her sales the year before. "And we need to beware of the time. Who knows what the girls will rope us into if we're late."

Annie's green eyes widened. "I completely forgot to think about themes! How embarrassing." She drained the last drops of coffee and took her mug and Alice's to the sink.

"Don't worry about it. There will be enough ideas from the others to prime the creative pump. Can I persuade you to take a few of the remaining molasses crinkles?"

"If I must. Mother and Gram both taught me the virtue of serving others." Annie took a small plate from a cabinet.

"Betsy loved my molasses crinkles too. Superb taste must run in the family." Alice arranged a pyramid of cookies on the plate and tucked the cloth back over the basket.

Annie placed a glass cake dome over the cookie plate. "I think it might have skipped a generation. Mother was known to eat crickets—and worse—on the mission field. And she enjoyed it!"

The two friends shuddered. "No cricket crinkles from me, though Boots might like them."

"Now there's a stocking-stuffer idea." Annie walked down the hall, with Alice following, stopping in the living room to grab her crochet tote bag. Almost empty and collapsing in on itself, the bag had a forlorn air about it. "Mary Beth's new project is coming at just the right time. I need something new to crochet."

"You'll have plenty of handwork to keep you busy when you're not organizing. Whatever theme is decided, the plan is to make as many items as possible to sell at Harvest on the Harbor."

"And to think there was a time not so long ago when I

didn't know what to do with myself!" For the first year after Wayne passed away, Annie could not imagine a full life would bloom again for her. Except for the love of her busy daughter and grandchildren, her days had been as sparse as the desert of West Texas. Her grandmother's death had changed that, leaving Annie with so much more than wonderful memories and the charming old Grey Gables. She had been gifted with a new sense of community and purpose.

When Annie and Alice arrived at A Stitch in Time, Mary Beth and Kate had their heads together behind a large box sitting on the front counter. "Look at these coconut-shell buttons," Kate marveled. "Lattice, embossed, flower-printed, abstract—and they're so light. I'm going to use these in my next jacket design."

Mary Beth nodded. "A nice addition to our horn, bone and bamboo buttons." She then noticed the two arriving club members. "We'll get started in a couple minutes. Peggy should be here soon."

Stella Brickson and Gwendolyn Palmer, the two knitters of the group, greeted Annie and Alice from their seats in the circle. Stella was working a sleeve on her size 4 straight needles.

"Stella, what a striking pattern!" Annie dropped her tote bag on a seat and drew closer to investigate. "Is that silk yarn?"

The eighty-three-year-old widow allowed a hint of a smile to cross her lips. "Yes, it's one hundred percent silk. There's a Japanese feather pattern around the cuffs and along the hem of the body too." She dipped her needles slightly to point at her knitting bag where a sleeveless tunic was neatly folded.

"Alice, that honey color would set off your hair gorgeously," Gwen commented with her usual gentle smile.

"Since I can't knit a stitch, I guess one of you two will have to make me a honey of a hat," said Alice.

Annie returned to her seat, making a mental note to ask Mary Beth to set aside some of that same yarn. She might not knit, but she knew her way around a crochet hook.

"You didn't start without me, did you?" Peggy's energetic voice preceded her to the circle of chairs.

"Well, if we did, we also started without Kate and Mary Beth," Alice teased as Peggy appeared in the circle.

"Annie!" Peggy hurried over and threw her arms around her surprised friend. "I don't know how I'll ever thank you enough! Emily twirled and twirled when we told her she won't have to stop her dance lessons this winter."

"Thank Wally," Annie said as she hugged back. "His lobster boat sold itself. All I did was bring the order list back to Stony Point."

Peggy dropped onto a chair. "And you didn't let on at all yesterday at the diner." She narrowed her eyes into a glare.

"Wally asked me to keep it a secret until he could tell you. If he hadn't, I would have given you every detail before the coffee even filled the mug. It was no easy feat, I tell you." All the ladies laughed, even Stella.

The last button box unpacked, Mary Beth and Kate joined the group. "It sounds like you've kept yourselves entertained while we finished up," said Mary Beth. "Are we ready to come up with an interesting theme for this year's Harvest on the Harbor? Annie, this is your first Harvest project. How about you start us off?"

Guilt flashed across Annie's face. "Umm, well ... I confess, I got occupied yesterday and forgot to think about it. But, being from the South, I'm rather partial to autumn leaves since we don't get much of that in Texas."

"Autumn leaves are a perfect idea," said Gwen.

"So perfect that we chose to do them last year," Mary Beth finished, "and it was a huge success. But you've got the idea, Annie, even if you were preoccupied."

"Were you working on a new mystery, by any chance?" asked Peggy. Annie's knack of becoming embroiled in mysteries that had started in the attic of Grey Gables had often been the source of both entertainment—and sometimes discomfort—to the community of Stony Point, and particularly the members of the Hook and Needle Club.

"No!" Annie threw up her hands. "I don't have time for a new mystery! Preparing for a visit from my family and working on the Harvest project is all I have time for."

"How about apples?" Peggy suggested. "The orchard owners inland would like that, I think." In her years working at The Cup & Saucer, Peggy had gotten to know the people who came to the Harvest on the Harbor celebration very well. She was also a huge fan of apple pie.

"Would that give enough scope for variety?" asked Mary Beth.

"We could do cornucopias," offered Kate. "That adds a little variety with both fruits and vegetables." She pursed her lips as she pictured the possibilities. "But I'm still not sure it's enough."

"I was thinking about scarecrows." Alice patted her sewing bag. "I found an adorable scarecrow cross-stitch pattern book last year at a flea market."

"I've heard that Wiscasset is hosting a scarecrow contest this year." Stella had not missed a stitch as she followed the discussion. "Might it seem like we're copying or competing? Wiscasset is our county seat, after all."

"Hmmm, that's something to think about," said Mary Beth. "Any other ideas that would compete less?"

"Kate's cornucopia idea has me thinking about the Pilgrims," said Gwen. "Harvesttime was so vitally important to them." As a member of the Daughters of the American Revolution, Gwen felt a strong connection to the early settlers of New England.

"How would a Pilgrim theme be worked out in needlecraft?" Peggy asked. "I guess I could use a Log Cabin quilt pattern. Would that be Pilgrimy enough?"

Stella lowered her knitting into her lap. "Drawing our theme from the past certainly fits the spirit of the day, but how would you like to do something a little more daring?"

All eyes were fixed on Stella. Although Stella had lived many years in New York City—and since she had enough money to pretty well do whatever she wanted to do—the club members didn't generally associate her with "daring."

"In my work with various museums over the years I've been fascinated with the culture and art of the American Indian tribes of New England. In the five years since I've been back in Stony Point, I've never seen any of the American Indian tribes of this area acknowledged for their contribution to the survival of the early settlers or their sacrifices during the Revolutionary War. Wouldn't the Harvest festival be an appropriate time to do that?" Stella lifted her knitting and added stitch by stitch. For a moment, the only sound to be heard in the circle was the clicking of needles.

"I, for one, love the idea." Alice was the first to give her opinion, not an uncommon occurrence. "Except, I know absolutely nothing about the American Indian tribes around here."

"I feel the same," added Kate. "I've seen some amazing patterns in native artwork, but I need to learn much more to do the project justice." The other women nodded their agreement.

Mary Beth turned to Stella. "Do you have suggestions of where we might find the guidance we need to do this successfully? It's an exciting project idea, and we'd want to do it well."

"That's right," said Peggy. "It would be embarrassing to get it wrong."

Stella nodded. "I would suggest the Abbe Museum in Bar Harbor. They have put together an impressive collection of Maine American Indian history, art, culture, and archaeology."

"Does this mean what I think it means?" Peggy grinned.

"Road trip!" The Hook and Needle Club answered in unison.

"I'll ask as soon as I get back to work about switching my days so I can go to Bar Harbor." Peggy gathered her things and stood up. "And I better get back to start buttering up the boss."

"Hey, for once we're investigating something other than one of Annie's mysteries!" Alice observed.

"Give her time." Kate winked. "She just got back into town." Laughter danced around the shop.

"The only two mysteries I'm working on for the foreseeable future are what crochet item I'm going to craft for the Harvest project and how to ready Grey Gables for two Texas cyclones named John and Joanna," Annie reassured them. "I'm starting on the second one as soon as I get home."

And she did.

4

Annie tightened the red bandanna that covered her hair as she gazed around the attic, that was brightened by the early afternoon sun. "Boots, where in this wild pandemonium of Gram's curiosities should I start?" Sitting at Annie's feet, Boots raised a dainty white paw for a quick clean. "Why are you bothering? You're going to pick up a lot of dust, if you stay up here long." She chuckled as Boots gently set the paw down, only to raise another one for similar treatment. "Fine, go ahead. It's your saliva." Annie's eyes again wandered from pile to pile. "How I wish this attic was as easy to tidy as your paws."

She decided to start by pinpointing the areas that seemed most likely to collapse under the impact of curious children. Some of the stacks appeared to defy gravity, forming shapes that would have impressed Solomon Guggenheim. Annie almost felt guilty to be modifying the delicate balances, but the safety of John and Joanna came first. She dove right in, disassembling and repositioning the first pile of objects which included a wire birdcage, an ancient camera tripod, and a tramp-art wall mirror with cracked glass. The pile was as tall as Annie.

That possible avalanche diverted, Annie moved on to her right, clapping dust off her hands. "Next time I come up, a dozen microfiber dust cloths are coming with me!" The next hulking silhouette belonged to a wooden rack with four shelves. The color of the oak wood whispered familiarity to Annie.

"Where have I seen you?" Annie's head tilted to one side in contemplation. "Ah! The kitchen, of course!" She lifted a flap of old linens draping over the side of the second shelf from the top. Embossed in black were the words: *Dresden Bakers Company, ME, 1912*. Annie pictured in her mind's eye that same shelf and the one above it filled with jars of home-canned goodness. When Annie first arrived each summer, she was greeted by the last two jars of rose-hip jelly. Betsy always made sure to save them for her granddaughter to savor on toast during the summer. In the last week before Annie had to return home for school in Texas, Annie and Betsy would pick the first batch of rose hips and make jelly.

Annie ran her fingers lightly along the wood, feeling as though she'd just found a long-lost friend. It had been years since the taste of rose-hip jelly had touched her tongue, but she could still taste the tangy sweetness. Like cheery sheep, beach roses ranged along the hill outside Grey Gables to the rocky shore. She realized it would only be a couple of weeks before the rose hips would be ripe enough for picking. The desire to introduce her grandchildren to that flavor of her own childhood charmed her.

"Now, Gram, I just have to figure out where you put the recipe." Annie's murmur had a rueful note to it. She knew that just because recipes would generally be thought of as a kitchen item didn't mean Betsy stored them there. At one time, books on cooking, gardening, and homesteading had lined the bottom shelf of the baker's rack, balancing the weight of the army of jars above. Now boxes of veterinarian tools and supplies that belonged to Annie's grandfather lay there instead.

The more she thought, the more she wanted to bring the baker's rack back to its former place in the large kitchen. While she might not fill the shelves with as many varieties of canned vegetables, Annie was determined to make a good showing of rose-hip jelly. The first step was to make sure the piece was still sturdy or if it was in need of repair. After making a visual check to ensure there weren't any glass items on the shelves, she placed her hands on either side of the rack. The shake from side to side told her the maker of the rack had built it to last.

Next, Annie decided to give it the "tip test." Scooting a box on the bottom shelf over a few inches, Annie placed her right foot in the space she had just made. Then, she pulled the rack forward just a little to test how easily the tall piece might topple with its load. The light pull barely moved the rack, so she kept her foot in place and jerked harder. Something launched off the top shelf, skimmed off Annie's head, and tumbled onto the dusty floorboards.

Boots padded over to sniff the object that had attacked Annie. "Maybe it would have been better if I'd looked at that top shelf more closely." Annie leaned over to scoop the box from under Boots' nose. Round and very light, the box was made from a dark, reddish-brown bark. Annie turned the box slowly in her hands; along the sides, etched deer and moose roamed among grass with birds flying overhead. The lid's rim was etched with vertical lines spaced about a half inch apart, and the top featured double geometric shapes and leaves.

When she had first picked up the box, it was so light Annie had assumed it was empty. But as she turned it to look at the designs she heard movement inside. Taking off the lid, Annie laid it gently on the soft stack of linens. She carefully drew out what was nestled inside. Tilted toward the afternoon sun coming in the attic window, light caught colorful beadwork. "How exquisite!" On a slightly faded black fabric background periwinkle blue and soft rose wildflowers bloomed among delicate green leaves. The long rectangle was less than three inches wide. "Hmmm, I wonder," Annie murmured. She gently lifted the beaded strip to her forehead to wrap the piece around her head. "Either I'm as big-headed as I am hard-headed, or this was not made for a head, even a child's head. A little lower, perhaps." The ends of the beautiful beadwork met around Annie's throat. "That's more like it."

She looked around for a mirror and remembered the broken tramp-art mirror in the pile she had just rearranged. Tilting the mirror for a better angle, Annie caught a look of herself and the beaded flowers adorning her neck. "Gram, how did this find its way to your attic?" Annie supposed it was silly to keep asking Betsy questions, but she always felt so close to her grandmother whenever she ventured up to the attic. She almost expected to see Gram winking at her from behind the old vanity in the corner, just like she used to when they played hide-and-seek together during Annie's first summer in Stony Point. And almost as though Betsy had whispered a reminder, sending it along on the sunbeams, Annie remembered there was something else in the intriguing box.

A folded sheet of paper was curled along the inside wall of the box. When Annie opened it, she realized the bottom third of the sheet had been torn. The writing was old-fashioned and finely flourished, much different from her own utilitarian script. Though not titled, the words on the page formed a poem—or at least part of a poem. Annie read aloud:

Sister Otter, water dancing
Sun splashes over circles you draw.
If love took you to desert dry,
Where would you dance?

Sister Rabbit, thicket thriving
Rain nurtures the chokeberries you eat.
If love took you to ocean deep,

There the lines ended, the words silenced in midthought. The handwriting revealed a writer who had been taught long before electric typewriters or computers. Was the poem copied as a penmanship exercise? Or had it flowed from heart to pen? Where was the rest of the page?

Betsy was well remembered as a person who loved beauty in all dimensions; Annie could not imagine her hiding away these pieces of art in her attic without a good reason. But what that reason could possibly be was beyond her. Annie tucked the poem back into the box, taking care to be gentle with the aging paper. The knowledge she had gained from her grandparents' love of antiques and her parents' international travel in their ministry convinced Annie the designs were not European, Asian, or African. Rubbing her finger over the texture of the wood, she decided her friends at the Hook and Needle Club might enjoy seeing the box and beadwork, and Annie hoped that between them all they could puzzle out their origin.

"Come on, Boots. I think we've had enough time up here for the day." Annie maneuvered her way through the attic maze to the door. Boot darted ahead, down to the second floor. Stopping in the cozy sitting room off her bedroom, Annie retrieved her camera from its perch on a double corner shelf. Boots meandered into the master bedroom, springing effortlessly onto the plump quilt of the bed. Annie set the box and camera on the chest of drawers. Her hands free, she rummaged through the shallow top drawers to find a white handkerchief. "This should do."

Spreading the handkerchief—all white except for a small navy blue monogrammed "CH" for Charles Holden, her grandfather's name, in one corner—on the quilt, Annie placed the beaded strip on it and took several photos. The box with the lid received the same treatment. Last, she took photos of the poem to highlight the style of handwriting. Boots remained a bored witness to her photographic efforts, renewing her interest in fur hygiene. After returning the camera to the sitting room, Annie sat down at the small writing desk to copy out the lines of the poem. Finally, she tucked the box, with its treasures nestled inside, into her tote bag.

A glance at the clock surprised her with the news that it was well past dinnertime. Too excited to sit nibbling crackers and cheese alone, she punched Alice's number into the phone. At Alice's cheery "Hello!" Annie blurted out, "Have you eaten dinner yet? I have something amazing to show you!"

"Lobster soufflé? Baked Alaska?" Alice replied.

"I said show you, not feed you. Besides, I've been in the attic all afternoon and totally forgot to plan for dinner," Annie admitted. She heard her friend chuckle.

"It just so happens that I made a delicious lemon tarragon roasted chicken earlier, and I'd be glad to share it."

"You are too nice to me, Alice. But why would you make a

whole chicken if you weren't already planning to have people over? Testing a new recipe for a Divine Décor party?"

"No, I actually made it for myself. See, this way I cook one night, and then I have several meals done for the rest of the week. And the recipe tastes as delicious cold as it does right out of the oven. It really comes in handy for those days when I'm double-booked with demonstrations."

"It also comes in handy when you have absent-minded friends next door. So when can you come?"

"Turn on the porch light, put on some tea, and I'll be there in a few minutes."

While Alice was spooning up the chicken, roasted potatoes, and vegetables, Annie brought the box down to the living room and put the kettle on to heat. She slipped out onto the porch to enjoy the sights and sounds of early evening, including the crunch of gravel under foot as Alice made her way to Grey Gables.

"So what is this amazing thing you have to show me?" Alice asked before she even made it to the porch steps. "I forgot to ask you on the phone. I'm far too easily distracted by food conversation."

"Something I found in the attic while I was organizing. And that's all I'm telling you until the tea water has boiled."

"Betsy's attic strikes again! Sounds like we might have spoken too soon this morning at the meeting." Alice grinned as she climbed the steps, holding the dish in both hands.

"I should know better by now, shouldn't I?" Annie said sheepishly as she held the door open for Alice. "But I have to admit, the timing of this is pretty cool. I'm making chai for myself. Would you like that or something else—chamomile, decaf Darjeeling, oolong?"

"I'll have the decaf Darjeeling. I don't know if I've seen a decaf variety before."

"The twins gave me a wonderful tea sampler for my birthday. I suspect they had a little help picking it out. But that doesn't stop me from thinking about them every time I have a cuppa." The friends could hear the kettle whistling as they entered the kitchen. On the counter next to the stove stood two small ceramic teapots, one blue with sailboats, and the other a soft green, dotted with dainty flowers. "Can you tell which twin picked out which pot?" Annie filled each infuser with tea and poured water from the kettle over it.

"Joanna definitely strikes me as a boat gal." Alice feigned total seriousness. "Now, are you going to show me the amazing find or not?" Alice tapped a foot and put her hands on her hips.

"It's in the living room," Annie gestured for Alice to follow her. "After a few hours of sorting and rearranging I came across Gram's old oak baker's rack. Remember that?"

Alice paused to think and then nodded. "Yes! She had it in the kitchen for years, loading it with jars and jars of food from her garden. That is, until after Charley died, and she became too weak for all that work. I think she had it moved to the attic so she wouldn't feel guilty about not being able to fill it up."

"That sounds like Gram, definitely," Annie agreed. "And she would never have been able to sell something that had such a large place in her daily life for so many years. Well, I want to bring that old rack back to the kitchen where it belongs and do my best to at least put up some rose-hip jelly in Gram's honor."

"A delicious idea," quipped Alice. "But seriously, what a

wonderful tradition to continue with your grandchildren. And if you find yourself with an extra jar or two, I can suggest a willing home for them. Especially if you have Betsy's recipe." She resisted the urge to smack her lips at the sweet memory of Betsy's jelly.

"We have a couple of weeks to find it before hip picking begins. Anyway, I wanted to check the stability of the rack to make sure it was still sturdy enough for frequent use. So I shook it and then rocked it. Look what slid off and bumped my head." Annie stepped away from where she stood in front of the rococo table, revealing the box.

"Whoa! Look at that workmanship." Alice knelt down to get a closer look. "The detail of the etchings blows me away." She ran the fingers of her right hand lightly over the deer, moose, and birds. "This is birch bark, in case you don't recognize it."

"I thought it might be. Remember, Gram and Grandpa took me all over Maine during my visits. Grandpa loved showing me all the flowers and trees that don't grow down in Texas. Do you think the box was made locally?"

"I think it could have been made in Maine," Alice replied, her eyes on the patterns of the box. "But birches grow in many other cold-weather areas. Russia, for instance. Not that I think this is Russian."

"There's more." Annie lifted the lid and gently retrieved the beaded piece. She laid it on the table right under Alice's eyes and watched the spark of delight flare even brighter.

"Oh, Annie, the artistry!" Alice said, her voice lowered in awe. "Just think. If you hadn't remembered the baker's rack or had just left it there, instead of testing it for a move downstairs, you may never have found these. You're going to show the other club members, aren't you?

Annie remembered her strong feeling of Gram's presence in the attic but didn't mention it to Alice. It would sound too much like an episode of Ghost Whisperer, and she was no Melinda Gordon. "Of course, I took some photos of the pieces. Oh, and a sheet of writing paper was tucked inside. A kind of poem was written on it in old-fashioned script. I copied down the words." She pulled the notepaper out of her jeans pocket and handed it to Alice. "The sheet was torn, so I don't know how the poem ends."

Alice stood up, her lips moving in concentration as she read the lines. "I've never heard these words, have you?"

"No, but I've never been a huge reader of poetry either, so that's not saying much. I'm planning to bring the photos and the poem copy on the road trip. Maybe one of the others have heard it before and can tell us how it ends and who wrote it."

"And maybe someone will know why those things were in the Holden's attic. This is going to be one rocking road trip!"

"Having the baker's rack project to keep me busy until next Tuesday is a blessing, or I think I'd go totally bonkers." Annie put the beadwork back in its nesting box. "The tea must be nice and strong now. Let's go eat!"

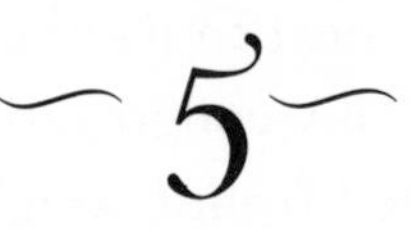

The moment Annie entered A Stitch in Time, Mary Beth greeted her with, "Did you bring those photos of your latest mystery?"

Annie patted her tote bag. "Of course I brought them. You've been tortured enough for one week, having to wait several days since Alice told you about them." Annie had been strict with herself, keeping to her plan of whipping Grey Gables lovingly into shape for Thanksgiving. She had known if she spent too much time in town, little would be accomplished before the road trip.

"Yes, I have been. So out with them, dear!" Mary Beth leaned over the counter and called, "Kate, Peggy, Gwen! Annie's brought the photos."

"Isn't Stella here?" It was a rare day when Annie could make it to the Hook and Needle Club meeting before its most veteran member.

"Stella is going to meet us at the museum. She told me she has a stop to make on the way," Mary Beth explained as the three other women came in from the meeting room.

Peggy squealed, "Oh, I just knew it wouldn't be long before another mystery came along! Let us see!" The gleam in their eyes told Annie that Kate and Gwen were as eager as Peggy.

Annie laid the photos in a line on the counter, showing

the box and lid, then the beadwork, and finally, the poem with her printed copy next to its photo. All four heads bent simultaneously like a tiny congregation called to prayer.

A soft gasp escaped from Gwen, "Oh, this beadwork is exquisite, Annie. Beadwork can be so tricky, and these seed beads look so tiny."

"Exquisite is exactly the word I thought, too, Gwen," Annie said.

"What perfect colors," Kate murmured. "The dark background makes them sparkle like fireworks at midnight."

"Have you seen these etchings on the box yet?" Peggy nudged Mary Beth's arm. "I don't think I'd be surprised if the crunchah jumped right off the bark and started galloping down the counter!"

"*Crunchah*?" Annie asked.

"You would probably say, 'cruncher,' Annie. It's a wicked big deer," Peggy informed the Texan.

"Annie," Mary Beth said, after carefully examining both box and lid, "do you have any idea what you have here?"

"Not exactly," admitted Annie. "Last night I wondered if Grandpa had made the box. But if I remember right, he enjoyed working with substantial blocks of wood. Something like this etching would have been too nerve-wracking for him. He had enough delicate surgery in his veterinarian practice."

"Perhaps we should discuss this on the drive," Kate suggested in her quiet voice, almost apologetically. "I'd hate to keep Stella waiting on us, if she arrives much before us."

"I cleaned out the backseats of the SUV, so we can all ride together," Mary Beth said. "You can chalk that up to a late summer miracle!" Mary Beth's vehicle was usually a rolling miniature version of her store, so the women were duly impressed by her efforts. Annie gathered up her photos, not bothering to put them back in her bag. She knew they'd all be discussing them for a fair portion of the ride.

Just as the group reached the door of the shop, Alice breezed in through it. "Whew! Made it by the skin of my teeth ... whatever that means. A new client called right as I was picking up my car keys. And wouldn't you know, at eight fifteen in the morning she was totally confused about the hostess gift program. Go figure." While Alice's voice sounded a bit harried, her eyes had not lost their usual twinkle.

"For her heroic efforts to get here, come hostess or high water, I think Alice should be the one to ride shotgun," declared Annie.

"Ayuh," Peggy said in agreement. The others nodded.

"Thank you. Thank you." Alice solemnly bowed to the group. "I will do my best to live up to this honor which you have bestowed upon me."

Mary Beth gave her a playful shove on her back. "Walk and talk, Alice, or you'll have Stella to answer to."

"Oh, we can't have that!" Alice strode to the passenger side of the SUV and climbed inside as soon as Mary Beth unlocked the doors. Once everyone was settled into their seats, Alice asked over her shoulder, "What do you think of Annie's photos? Does anyone recognize any of the items?"

"As I was going to tell Annie before we left, I'm convinced the etched birch bark is an American Indian design because I've seen some other birch-bark boxes and baskets with similar types of construction over the years. But I couldn't tell you where they came from, or when they were made." Mary Beth kept her eyes on the road as she spoke, guiding the SUV along Main Street to head north on U.S. Highway 1.

"I've read a couple of articles about the beading traditions among American Indian tribes, but I've never seen anything like Annie's piece before. Stunning work," said Kate.

"Annie, may I see the writing and poem copy?" asked Gwen. Annie handed the photo and poem over the seat to Gwen.

"Read it for us, Gwen," said Peggy, who was gazing at the photo of the box lid.

Gwen did as she was asked, her clear voice precisely enunciating each word with the exception of the words "sister" and "otter." Those she pronounced as her Maine-rooted family always had, "sistah" and "ottah." Annie hid a smile, thinking it wouldn't be too hard to teach Gwen a good Southern drawl, if she had a mind to learn it.

Gwen turned around after finishing the poem. "Peggy, you were in school more recently than the rest of us. Do you remember this poem from any of your classes?"

A light blush dusted Peggy's cheeks. "Well, no. But I was busy with cheerleading … and convincing Wally that he really was the only guy I wanted to date. Made it hard to concentrate in class."

"I, for one, am thankful for all your hard work," said Alice. "I can't imagine Stony Point without the Carson family."

"I agree. The Carsons are an important part of our community," said Gwen. She lifted the photo in her hand, waving it gently. "I'm looking at the photo with the handwriting. My guess is that this was written no later than the turn of the century—the twentieth century, that is. It reminds me of some of the DAR displays I've seen, as well as my father's family Bible. The entries from the Civil War years used flourishes similar to this handwriting."

"My first reaction was that it was over a century old too." Annie couldn't help staring out the window as she spoke—the highway to Bar Harbor always delighted her with its scenery. "Which leaves me wondering if the box and its contents were already at Grey Gables when Gram and Grandpa bought it. Or did they buy them at an antique store or craft show?"

"Are you sure they're not part of your family's history? Maybe the Holdens brought the pieces with them when they moved in," Kate said.

"I've thought about that. But one of the things I loved doing every summer I visited was sitting next to Grandpa while he whittled on the porch of Grey Gables. As he turned the wood in his hands, he would tell me stories about the Holden family. How Justinian Holden had come to New England from Lancashire in England in the early 1630s, and how the family eventually settled in Maine. He told me about all sorts of folks in our family line, some noble and some rascals. He firmly believed there should be no such things as skeletons in the family closet." Annie sighed. She missed Grandpa.

"Maybe they came from Betsy's side," Peggy said, her cheeks now back to their usual hue.

"But Gram was the same way as Grandpa; she liked to tell family stories too, usually while we were picking rose hips or walking on the beach, looking for sea glass. I'd go home chock-full of stories of Gram's family from Scotland, and I loved it. Mother and Father told me stories too, but mostly stories from their mission work. I simply have a hard time believing that Gram wouldn't have shared such beautiful artifacts, if they held a place in our family's history." Annie missed them all.

Mary Beth smiled up into the rearview mirror and spoke softly, "Yes, you're right, Annie. Both Betsy and Charlie were like that."

"They were safe confidants for those who needed someone to talk to," Alice continued the theme, "but they were open books about themselves."

"Which leads us right back to a big fat mystery," Peggy proclaimed.

"I guess we can just pack away the questions until we get to the museum. Hopefully, someone there will have more information that will shed some light." Annie gathered the photos and poem that Peggy, Gwen and Kate handed her, tucked them back into her tote, and settled down into her seat to soak in the beauty of the small towns, rocky shore and wildflower fields they traveled past.

****

"We're almost there. I've just turned onto Mount Desert Street." Mary Beth's voice pried its way into Annie's reveries. Annie sat up straighter and peered out the window again.

Bar Harbor featured a village green, not much different from Stony Point's town square, even down to the gazebo shape and color. But Annie had spent enough time in the small Maine town to realize each community had its own unique combination of spirit, history, and personality. Just past the green on the left, Annie saw a red and gold flag waving in front of a white shingle-style building with dark green trim. "Oh, there it is! What a charming building!" she exclaimed.

"The building has the feeling of the summer homes of families like the Vanderbilts or Carnegies, only smaller, doesn't it?" said Gwen. She closed the book she'd been reading.

"Much smaller." Kate carefully gathered the crochet she had been working on during the ride and slipped it into a bag. She bent over to slide it under the seat. "But I like it. Makes me wonder what's hiding in the dormers."

Peggy started to make her way out of the van but stopped, pointing out the window. "There's Stella's Lincoln Continental, heading back down Mount Desert. Looks like Jason has already dropped Stella off."

"Stella probably hasn't been here long, then. That's a relief," Alice joked, wiping imaginary sweat from her forehead. She slid her purse over a shoulder and jumped out of the SUV.

The group walked past the stone and metal museum sign. The bright flag swayed in the soft breeze. Peggy stopped to watch it for a moment. "The red and gold on the flag really pops. Whatever design I find, I hope those colors will work with it."

"I'm partial to how they created the logo with the cutouts in metal," said Kate. "The tree would lend itself beautifully to crochet."

Annie paused to say over her shoulder, "Kate, just about anything would end up beautiful if you made it in crochet. And I'm not just saying that so you'll teach me new techniques." Kate smiled her thanks.

Entering the museum, the first person they saw was

Stella. She stood before the admissions desk, deep in discussion with the young woman behind it. A broad smile on her face, the woman handed Stella a small stack of brochures. Stella nodded her thanks and then turned to greet the other Hook and Needle Club members.

"Rose tells me we've come on a good day. Both the curator of collections and the curator of education are on-site today and available for any questions we may have." Stella handed a brochure to everyone.

"Great! Maybe they will know something about the items Annie found in her attic," Alice said. "You haven't seen the photos yet, have you, Stella? Perhaps you'll remember them!"

"I don't know that I can be much help." Stella turned to Annie. "The attic has revealed another mystery, has it?"

Annie dug the photos and poem out of her purse. "Do you remember ever seeing these or hearing Gram talk about them?" She fanned the photos out like a hand of cards and extended them to Stella.

Settling her sensible reading glasses onto her nose, Stella thoroughly examined each of the photos and read the poem portion. She shook her head. "Sorry to say, I don't. That beadwork looks extraordinary, and I can't imagine why Betsy would not have displayed it prominently at Grey Gables." A shadow passed over her features, a hint of sorrow in her eyes. "But, as you know, there were decades when I was not a part of her life, through my own foolishness. I wasn't even living in Maine again until five years ago. I would assume she came into possession of these things during that time. How odd she never showed them to the other members of the handcraft community." Stella handed the photos back to Annie. "Do make sure you show these to one of the curators before we leave today. I am sure she would be helpful. Both curators are meticulous in their research and knowledge of American Indian culture and art. Rose mentioned that a good time would be around two o'clock this afternoon."

"That gives us plenty of time to look around," Peggy said to Annie as she unfolded her brochure. "Where should we start?" After sitting more than two hours in Mary Beth's SUV, Peggy was ready for some movement. By this time of day at The Cup & Saucer she would have already walked miles.

"Every artist or craftswoman finds her inspirations in different ways," Stella observed. "I should think it would be best to allow each person to go wherever she will and then meet back at an appointed time."

Mary Beth consulted her watch. "It's almost eleven. How about we meet back here at one o'clock, and then we can go grab a bite to eat before coming back for Annie's discussion with the curators?" With nods and murmurs of agreement, the members of the Hook and Needle Club spread out, a crafty SWAT team tracking down inspirations.

6

Two hours later, the seven women gathered together again with over-stimulated brains and empty stomachs. The brisk walk to Galyn's Restaurant was rejuvenating and influenced the unanimous decision to eat lunch on the porch overlooking Frenchman Bay rather than in the dining room. After ordering drinks and sustenance as met each woman's fancy, they settled back in their chairs to enjoy the breeze and the sounds of seabirds, water, and boats of every imaginable type coming and going on the bay.

"Does anyone else feel even more the weight of responsibility to do our theme justice now that we've spent these past hours at the museum?" asked Alice.

Peggy nodded. "I sure do. This project is much more serious than making a quilt for Emily. It's hard to go wrong with that; I just have to make sure there are lots of pink and purple in it." Her left hand with its lobster-tipped fingers toyed with the sweetener packets, lifting each color separately as though she was taking inventory for restocking. "But I saw quite a few things that gave me ideas … as long as I don't mess them up."

"Peggy, you've been quilting for some time now," said Mary Beth. "I've seen your work. I know you'll create something that will do justice to the theme."

"It's hard to argue with you, Mary Beth, since it's your

project. But I sure hope you're right." Peggy's hand moved on to straightening the other condiments.

"I definitely know now that there is so much I *don't* know," asserted Annie. She paused and smiled at the waiter as he placed a cup of tea before her, setting a miniature pewter pitcher of milk beside it, and made his way around the table delivering the other drinks.

After he disappeared into the indoor dining room, she turned to Stella. "I can't thank you enough for suggesting this museum visit, Stella. The exhibits and museum shop filled me with ideas." Stella nodded and gently smiled, acknowledging Annie's thanks. "But how to narrow all the possibilities into one piece!" Annie exclaimed.

"Did anyone find something you definitely want to use in your work?" asked Alice.

"As Annie said, there are so many intriguing and beautiful options." Kate's voice was soft as usual, but enthusiasm bubbled in it. "I was inspired by the tree cutout on the museum's sign, and after reading about the importance of the ash and other trees to the Maine tribes, I think I'm going to use a tree design. Perhaps in a shawl."

Gwen sipped her water with lemon. "Annie, did you see the birch-bark handkerchief box? The style of etching is quite similar to your box."

"Yes! I wrote some notes on that." Annie rummaged through her purse for the small notebook she always kept with her. Flipping through the pages she came to her museum notes. "Ah, here it is. 'The handkerchief box was made by a Passamaquoddy man named Tomah Joseph around 1900,'" Annie read. "So, maybe my box was made by a

Passamaquoddy artist. But I think other Maine tribes also made things with etched birch bark. I hope the curator will be able to narrow it down. Did you see that basket with the rose made from porcupine quills? I can't imagine that's as easy to do as crochet!"

"It looked like fine embroidery!" said Alice. "I'd love to do something with that kind of look, but I don't think cross-stitch is the right medium. But there was a chair that had decorative panels with quillwork too, and the pattern would fit cross-stitch perfectly. I might use those panels for my inspiration."

"It sounds like our road trip has done its job," declared Mary Beth. "With the history we've learned, and various items we've seen, this year's Harvest on the Harbor project is sure to be interesting—and profitable for the Thanksgiving Turkey Giveaway." The sound of the door opening onto the porch caught her attention, and Mary Beth glanced over her shoulder. "I think it's time for us to enjoy our lunch!" Nearby, the waiter opened up a tray table with one hand and placed the large tray of food on top.

The conversation changed direction and slowed down considerably as the women focused attention on their lunch choices. Lobster bisque, chicken focaccia, spinach salad, crab cakes, and quiche all disappeared in good time, as did a round of blueberry-apple crisp. Satisfied and revived, by two o'clock they returned to the Abbe Museum.

Checking with Rose again at the information desk, Annie was directed to the office of Kezi Vance, curator of collections. Tucked in a corner of the lower-level hallway dominated by the Abbe's archaeology lab, the curator's door was open. A woman with dark, medium-length layered hair sat behind a cluttered desk, her right cheek resting in her right hand as she concentrated on the chunky catalog that had won her immediate attention.

Annie lightly knocked on the door frame. "Excuse me, are you Ms. Vance?"

The woman's head shot up like a guilty daydreamer in elementary school. But her eyes, which reminded Annie of Alice's molasses crinkle cookies, were merry rather than ashamed. Bounding up out of her chair, she extended her hand to Annie.

"Oh, please, do call me Kezi. How may I help you?"

"I'm Annie Dawson. I have inherited a house from my grandmother, Betsy Holden, and I found some items in the attic that have me very curious. I've brought several photos and am hoping you might be able to give me some information on them."

"Betsy Holden?" The curator peered at Annie a little more closely. "The 'Betsy Original' Betsy Holden?"

No matter how many times Annie heard similar reactions to Gram's name, it never failed to startle her. Her smiled deepened. "Yes, that Betsy Holden."

"Her landscapes are some of the finest in fiber arts I've ever seen. And she did such a service to the whole state in starting the New England Stitch Club. We have a chapter right here in Bar Harbor." Kezi waved her hand toward a leather-upholstered captain's chair in front of the desk. "Please, sit down."

"Thank you. Along with being creative and loving, Gram was also quite a collector, and her attic overflows with enough random objects to fill a merchant ship. Last week, as I was doing some organizing, I found three items that have me puzzled as to their origins." Annie reached into her purse, drawing out the photos. First, she handed over the photos of the birch-bark box. "During my childhood and teen years, I spent summers at Gram's house, but I don't remember seeing this. It's beautiful."

Kezi nodded as she looked over the photos. "Have you looked at our exhibits yet?"

"Yes, our Hook and Needle Club came this morning to look for inspirations for projects we're working on for our town's Harvest celebration. Among the many astounding pieces, I saw a handkerchief box that had a similar style of construction, from what I could see. I wondered if it was made around the same period as Gram's or if Gram's box is a reproduction."

"It would be easier to make a definite call, if I could see the actual box." Kezi reached into the top drawer of her desk and took out a magnifying glass. Passing it slowly over the photos, she continued, "There are subtle variations of color and often definite progressions in patterns of decoration between birch-bark items from the past, and from reproductions or more contemporary designs, reflecting cultural change."

She reached behind her where a long but squat bookshelf covered the wall below her office window. Taking a binder from the top shelf, she flipped through the plastic-sleeved pages. When she found the pages she was looking for, she handed the notebook to Annie. "That page shows the handkerchief box you mentioned. It was made around the year 1900. You can see that the craftsman created a traditional American Indian—particularly Passamaquoddy—camp scene on the lid, and along the sides, depicted things that were important to the Passamaquoddy life: canoes, animals, plants. Now turn to page fifty-six."

Annie found the page. It contained a birch-bark box that was round like the one she had found in her attic. "The color of this box looks lighter," she said. Kezi smiled, encouraging her to continue. "And although it has a fish carved into the lid, it almost looks more like a modern logo, when compared to the handkerchief box. But it's so striking!"

"Both of the boxes were made by Passamaquoddy artists, but one was made in 2007 and one more than a hundred years before. Which of the two looks more like the box you found?"

"Oh, definitely, the handkerchief box."

"I agree. Again, I could make a more positive identification if I had the box here. But I'm pretty confident that what you have found is a Passamaquoddy birch-bark box made sometime before or at the turn of the twentieth century. And it looks like it's in gorgeous condition."

"Inside the box I found two more things. This is one." Annie extended the photos of the beadwork across the desk.

Kezi's molasses-crinkle eyes widened in delight, and her mouth puckered to let out a soft whistle. "*Wow.* And I thought the box was a wonderful find for an attic. This is truly an amazing treasure, Annie."

"What is it exactly?" Annie leaned forward in anticipation.

"From these photos, it would seem that you have possession of a regalia collar. Such collars were worn only during very special tribal gatherings."

"Which tribe do you think it might have come from?"

"Several tribes in Maine and New England were master beadworkers. Those in the Micmac and Maliseet tribes used their beadwork not only for personal items but also for the non-native markets. They made beaded tea cozies, watch pockets, purses, and other things for which they found buyers."

"So it's possible that my grandparents bought the collar from an art show or market?" Annie tried to ignore the seed of disappointment sprouting inside her.

"That could be possible, but there's another scenario I think might be more likely." Kezi pulled another binder off the shelf. She selected a page and propped it open on the desk at an angle so that both she and Annie could see. On the page was a photo of an American Indian woman wearing a beaded collar, as well as a beaded hat with a wide brim and several long necklaces. The facing page showed a man with a feather headdress and wide collar with complex beading draped over his shoulders. "This woman was of the Passamaquoddy tribe. The man was a Penobscot chief. Unlike the Micmac and Maliseet tribes, the Passamaquoddy and Penobscot generally only used their beadwork for personal regalia items. Each person developed their own regalia designs, and they were very special personal items that were generally kept within each family, passed down from generation to generation."

"Can you tell which tribe this collar was from?" Annie asked.

"The color choices, shape and width of the collar fits very well with many of the Passamaquoddy collars I have seen, including the one in this binder. I would say the fact that it was kept in a Passamaquoddy box is instructive as to its origins, except you don't know how the box came to be in your possession." She gathered Annie's photos together in a stack and passed them to their owner across the desk. "If you feel comfortable about it, I'd love for you to bring the items in one day for me to take a closer look at them. But I have some confidence that the collar is of Passamaquoddy heritage, as is the box." Kezi slipped the two binders back in their places on the shelf.

"Thank you for your time and help," Annie said as she stood to leave. "I don't know why Gram had these gems hiding in her attic, but I'm going to try to find out."

"When you've solved the mystery, please let me know what you found." The phone on Kezi's desk began to beep. "If you'll excuse me, I need to answer this."

Annie nodded and waved her final thanks. As she walked down the hall, she could hear Kezi saying, "Kezi Vance, how may I help you?" No sooner had Annie stepped through the door into the front hall, her friends surrounded her.

"Did the curator help?" Alice asked.

"What did she tell you?" Peggy chimed in at the same time. Gwen and Stella looked at each other as though they were being indulgent with young children, but Annie knew they were just as interested as the others.

"Let's go out into the courtyard," Annie suggested, not wanting to disturb the other museum visitors. Once out in the fresh air, Annie revealed what she had learned from the curator.

"A Passamaquoddy regalia collar," Peggy said. "What in the world would Betsy be doing with one of those?" Her bangs shifted across her eyes as she shook her head in wonder.

"And neither she nor Charlie ever mentioned any American Indian heritage to you. That does seem quite mysterious," said Kate.

"Did the curator have any information on the poem you found?" asked Stella.

"I never had the chance to show her the poem," Annie admitted. "We were caught up in the other two things, and then she had to answer a phone call. But I think I'll be paying a visit to the Stony Point Library tomorrow to see if I can find anything out about the poem."

"This was the best Hook and Needle Club road trip ever," Alice declared. "We found tons of ideas *and* another mystery!" The other members all agreed. Even Annie.

"And neither she nor Charlie ever mentioned any American Indian heritage to you. That does seem quite mysterious," said Kate.

"Did the curator have any information on the poem you found?" asked Stella.

"I never had the chance to show her the poem," Annie admitted. "We were caught up in the other two things, and then she had to answer a phone call. But I think I'll be paying a visit to the Stony Point Library tomorrow to see if I can find anything out about the poem."

"This was the best Hook and Needle Club road trip ever!" Alice declared. "We found tons of ideas and another mystery!" The other members all agreed. Even Annie.

7

Annie strode up the steps of the Stony Point Library, grateful that the uncertain economy had not resulted in hours being trimmed off the community mainstay. Patting a pillar as she passed, she wondered how she would have concentrated on anything else if the library had not opened first thing in the morning. So many community libraries in Maine were having to trim time or days from their weekly operations.

I need to send some notes of appreciation to Ian and the town commissioners for their hard work on the budget, she thought. *How they've managed to keep the library salaries and expenses the same is a miracle of management.* Annie pulled open the glass door. Note-writing would have to wait. Today was to be devoted to the mystery of the poem.

Even at the end of summer, when it might be expected that folks would be spending as much time as they could on the water or beach, or that teens would be sleeping late before school started up again the following week, the Great Room had an air of quiet occupation. An interesting mix of patrons draped across chairs reading magazines or with books spread before them on the oval tables. But Annie was confident she would be able to snag a computer in the Reference Room after looking through the poetry books the library had in circulation.

Annie tracked down an empty computer devoted to searching the library's collection. Clicking on the "Search by Topic" button, she typed "Passamaquoddy poetry" into the box and clicked "Search." A long list scrolled down the page. Excitement began to stir until she took a closer look at the items on the list. Starting with "passing," the list included passion, Passover, pasta, and pastel, among others. Not one Passamaquoddy.

Maybe I'm being too specific. Annie thought as she went back to the search box and typed "American Indians poetry." This time "first words" topped the list, followed by fiscal policy, fish, fish as food, fisheries, and Fishers, as in Jonathan Fishers. With an entire page filled with fiction and nonfiction dedicated to fisheries alone, it wasn't hard to deduce the importance of marine resources to the state of Maine. But it wasn't helping solve this mystery. Annie glanced around to make sure another patron didn't need the online catalog. Other than some young children scampering toward the Children's Room with their mothers frantically whispering for them to slow down, everyone else seemed to have found what they were looking for or were quietly perusing the rows of books in the stacks.

Annie thought back to the conversation she had had with her friends the day before as they described their education about Maine's American Indian tribes. Her fingers tapped on the keyboard again. "Maine Indians." This time the list showed four individual nonfiction books. Two were pamphlets from the early 1900s, one entitled "The Problem of the Red-Paint People" and the other, "Indian Tribes of Maine." *The Penobscot* appeared to be the only book the library held on local American Indians. Although there was nothing in the listing to indicate the book explored the subject of American Indian poetry, Annie jotted down the call number. An advanced search reaped only repeated harvests of "unable to find results based on criteria."

She had been sitting long enough. Annie found the book on the Penobscot tribe, double-checked where in the Dewey decimal sections poetry was located, and dove back into the stacks. Longfellow, Edna St. Vincent Millay, May Sarton leaned against Frost, Hughes, and other names Annie didn't recognize. Determined not to miss a single poetry book, she stooped and tilted her head to read every spine, pulling out any book with the remote possibility of containing the poem she was seeking. She felt like a swimmer draining water out of her ear.

Nothing.

Time to search the Web, Annie thought as she gathered her things and walked through the arch to the Reference Room. Though the room had filled considerably while Annie searched the stacks, one of the many computers was still free. Smiling at the few people who looked up as she walked by, Annie settled in at the computer and clicked on the Internet icon. Accessing Google, she typed in the words of the first line of the poem: "sister otter water dancing." While the search engine proclaimed "about 280,000 results," those results were not helpful. From many mentions of a children's television show, *PB&J Otter,* to animal profiles from naturalists to adult monikers for social-networking websites she didn't recognize, Annie scanned pages and pages. She typed in other lines from her copy, but the poem was not to be found.

"Well, that certainly sped up the process," muttered Annie, a little disappointed. Her eyes darted around the room to make sure she hadn't disturbed anyone. She'd been so intent on her search, she'd almost forgotten where she was. The Stony Point Library Reference Room was beginning to feel too much like home. Mentally crossing off the possibility that the poem had been copied from a published piece, Annie felt comfortable with her conclusion that the poem had been a private composition. How to discover who the author was and why the verse was in Gram's attic was another story.

Not yet satisfied with her research for the day, Annie switched her focus. As teenagers came and went after posting statuses on their Facebook pages, and adults checked movie schedules or sent employment applications, she cast a line to see if she could hook some more information on the Passamaquoddy people. Her second effort was more successful than her first. In addition to links from the Abbe Museum, state government, newspaper, and various cultural websites were sources to be explored. She even found links for an old Disney movie, *Pete's Dragon*. So that was why something had been buzzing in the back of her memory when she had looked at the exhibits at the museum. She had heard the word Passamaquoddy sung and spoken when LeeAnn and she had watched the movie on video together so many years ago.

With the hint of a smile hovering around her mouth, Annie began to read and read. At times there was little to smile about in the stories of devastation by new diseases brought to the land by European settlers—her own ancestors—or the neglect of government-paid employees and land agents. Then she stumbled on photos of art pieces that delighted her, and a video showing a Passamaquoddy artist weaving with nimble hands. She might have read on until Grace Emory, Josephine Booth, or whoever was scheduled to be the last staff member to leave that day came to shut down the computers. But her stomach had other plans, growling louder and louder until Annie was sure she was bothering others in the room.

Reluctantly she closed out the Google website and packed up her notebook and pen. As she walked across the Great Room, she waved to Grace who was behind the front desk, scanning books that had been returned. On her way down the porch steps she realized she had not checked out *The Penobscot* as she had planned. It was sitting tucked next to the computer. Reassuring herself that she would have plenty of time to stop in at the library after lunch, she continued on to cross Oak Lane, heading for The Cup & Saucer.

Annie thought she would be eating at a time when free booths were hard to come by, but when she pulled the door open, she was surprised at the low volume of conversation. Noting the amount of open seating, she glanced at the clock hanging beneath the high shelf populated with ivy-filled giant teacup planters. "Three o'clock!" Annie couldn't hold in her gasp.

A familiar chuckle reached her ears from the second booth from the door. Ian Butler leaned out and waved to Annie.

"Mysteries can be time hogs, and I hear you found a doozy." Ian slid out of the booth. "Want to share with me what you found over a late lunch, Annie?"

Annie patted her tote bag. "I'd love to, Ian. In fact, I was thinking of you at the library this morning." Realizing too late how that might sound, she hurried on before the mayor could comment. "When I was in Wiscasset before my trip, I saw signs on the library door stating the new hours of operation. The town has had to cut the hours due to the economy. I was wondering today what magic you and the town commissioners have conjured to keep our Stony Point Library open regular hours, and without staff reductions too."

"Are you wondering what 'we'ves gots in our pocketses?" Ian's voice morphed into a high-pitched, nasally rendition of one of Tolkien's fantasy creatures from *The Lord of the Rings* movies.

"Not exactly, Mr. Gollum. But I do appreciate your efforts very much. I wanted to make sure I thanked you. And the other officials, of course."

Before Ian could respond, Lisa, the swing-shift waitress, hurried over to take Annie's order. "Hi, Annie, You're really late today. What can I get for you?"

"I'm late and starving! And I'm also craving a Cobb salad with a cup of tea."

"Coming right up." Lisa handed the order over to the cook and began refilling the condiments at each table in preparation for the dinner crowd.

Ian leaned forward. All signs of Gollum were erased, leaving just a curious man. "Now, please tell me what you've found!"

"What? Haven't you been given a detailed description already?" Annie couldn't imagine the Hook and Needle Club members being able to keep the information to themselves after the trip.

"Not much," Ian insisted. "And I'm sure it was painful for Peggy and Mary Beth too. With the end of the tourist season and the transition to autumn come lots of meetings. Which is why I was almost as late to lunch as you were. Peggy was already gone."

Annie nodded. "She's probably working a split shift today."

"Mary Beth charged out of the store when she saw me coming for lunch. She gasped out that she'd given Kate some time off to take Vanessa shopping for school clothes, so she couldn't properly get me up to speed on the new mystery. Instead she left me with the command to 'look at Annie's photos!' Then she threw up her hands and darted back into the shop. She must have gotten a phone call or something."

"That does sound painful for Mary Beth." Annie smiled at the thought as Lisa brought her tea with a wedge of lemon and a honey bear. She pulled the photos from her tote bag and placed them before Ian. As her friend examined the photos as carefully as he did the town budget, Annie squeezed the lemon into her tea and followed it with a quick squeeze of honey. After a refreshing sip she continued.

"The birch-bark box was tucked away on the top shelf of a baker's rack. The beadwork and the torn notepaper were inside it. I don't remember ever seeing them during my summers with Gram. Do they look familiar to you at all?"

Ian slowly shook his head, his eyes still fixed on the photos. "No, I'm sorry to say they don't. I have seen birch-bark boxes and baskets in various places around Maine, but the designs were different. This one looks quite old."

"Kezi Vance, the curator of collections at Abbe Museum thinks all the items are dated at least from the turn of the twentieth century, and quite possibly earlier."

"What exactly is this?" Ian lightly tapped the edge of the photo showing the beadwork.

"Kezi was very confident that it's an American Indian regalia collar for a woman. She thinks it was most likely made by a Passamaquoddy woman."

"It's beautiful. The craftswoman would have been worthy of the Hook and Needle Club." Ian paused. "I know you've found some pretty amazing things in the attic, but I'm having a hard time accepting that Betsy would keep something like this hidden."

"You're not the only one, Ian. Not even Stella has seen the box or collar before. Gram and Grandpa told me story after story about our family's heritage without any mention of American Indian tribes. It just wouldn't be like them, if these are family heirlooms."

"What if Betsy discovered it late, not long before she died?"

"Then I think she would have shared it with *someone*—Alice or Mary Beth or even Kate. And I think especially she would have shared it, somehow, with me." Annie took a deep breath, wondering if the guilt she felt was earned. "I couldn't visit as often as I wanted in those last years, with running the dealership with Wayne and all, but I was always close with Gram." Annie stopped when her voice caught and lowered her head.

Ian reached his hand across the table and gently placed it under Annie's chin. "Hey," he said softly, lifting her chin to look her in the eyes. "You're right, Annie. Betsy would have shared it with you, no matter what or when."

"You're just saying that so this overly emotional woman will get a grip," Annie turned her head away from Ian's cupped fingers to dig into her tote for a tissue. She dabbed at her eyes.

"No, I'm saying it because your point makes complete sense. Besides, I have much more interesting techniques for overly emotional people of both genders, developed from years of on-the-job-training."

Lisa stepped quietly over to the table with Annie's Cobb salad and a roll. "Just let me know if you need more dressing or tea." Annie had no doubt Lisa had heard enough of their conversation to pass it on to Peggy. She could only shake it off and focus on her meal. Maybe that was the source of her unexpected emotional roller coaster—low blood sugar.

"Did you read the lines of the poem I copied?" Annie redirected the conversation before taking a bite of her salad. "Have you ever read anything like it?"

Ian read the lines again. "I'm beginning to feel like a broken record, but no, I haven't."

"I spent time at the library looking for any poetry book with that poem in its collection, or any reference to the lines on the Internet. Came up empty. But something surprised me," Annie said before taking another bite. With each bite she realized just how hungry she was. If she'd been home with only Boots for company, she would have wolfed it down in record time.

"What was that?"

"I had to work hard to find any books on American Indian

tribes in Maine. Finally I searched for Maine Indians and still came up with only two pamphlets and one nonfiction book on the Penobscot. That's it. No poetry or even story collections at all. With Stony Point's proud history, I expected more, I guess."

"I have to admit, I've not had those issues brought up to me, and I haven't thought about them even in my years as mayor, or when I was growing up here," said Ian, looking pensive.

"Maybe that's why Stella suggested the American Indian theme for Harvest on the Harbor. It was a way to bring them up. I'm fascinated with what I'm learning." Annie shifted her empty teacup to the edge of the table to make it easier for Lisa to give her a refill. "After the poetry and literature book search came up empty, I turned to the Internet. I still didn't find references to any of the lines of the poem, which leads me to conclude that it was a personal composition. But I found several places to learn more about the Passamaquoddy tribe and other Maine American Indian tribes."

Ian abruptly moved his head forward. "Why didn't I think of this sooner?! Annie, I know who you should talk with! Oh, sorry to interrupt."

"Interruptions are allowed for special cases, and this is one of them. Who do you think could help?" Annie asked eagerly, putting her fork down.

"There's a member of the Passamaquoddy tribe right here in town. His name is Cecil Lewey, and he lives at Ocean View Assisted Living. My brother Todd introduced him to me years ago. Let me call him first, but I'm sure he'd be pleased to talk with you. I'll call you as soon as I know."

"Oh, Ian, I can't thank you enough. Maybe he'll recognize the patterns on the box or the beadwork, or even know the artist!" Annie picked up her cup of tea in salute. "Here's to late lunches and public servanthood."

8

The next morning Annie's answering machine was blinking at her when she came in from a morning walk on the beach. She deposited the two new pieces of sea glass—one amber and one blue—into the sweetmeat dish before listening to the recorded message.

"Good morning, Annie!" boomed Ian's voice. "I spoke with Cecil Lewey earlier, and he would very much like to visit with you. If you're free today, he'll be available. Keep me posted on the mystery."

Boots strolled in as the message was playing and rubbed against Annie's denim-covered legs. Squatting, Annie ran a hand down Boots's back and gave her a good thorough chin and head rub. The cat had made it quite plain that she had not appreciated Grey Gables being empty so long yesterday and guilt lingered in the back of Annie's mind.

"If I knew you'd behave, I'd bring you with me," she told Boots. "But you have to admit you're a bit unpredictable at times, even for a cat. And Cecil might be allergic to cats." Boots stared at Annie, a furry statue. "I promise to stay home with you tonight." Boots looked none too convinced, but at least she did not try to block Annie's way upstairs to shower and change for the trip to Ocean View Assisted Living.

An hour later, Annie's Malibu was pulling up to the security gate of the facility. A white van with the name of an electrician emblazoned on the sides was stopped ahead of Annie's car, the driver talking to a man dressed in a polo shirt with the Ocean View logo stitched on the pocket. Looking around as she waited, Annie noticed a familiar Cadillac sedan pull up behind her. She smiled and waved into her rearview mirror at Gwendolyn Palmer. The van rumbled forward. Annie turned into the visitors' parking lot and, as she slid out of her car, Gwen steered her car into the space next to her.

"Hello, Annie!" Gwen's hair, slacks, and sweater set were impeccable. Annie knew the interior of her sedan was also. "Are you coming for the volunteer training? I'm helping Nora with the training session today."

"They picked the perfect assistant with all your experience, Gwen," said Annie, "but to answer your question, no; I'm here to visit a resident." The two friends followed the wide flagstone walkway to the front doors.

"Oh, who are you visiting?"

"Cecil Lewey." Annie pulled the right side of the large double door open, noticing that the colorful summer wreath that had hung there had been replaced with an artistic arrangement of dried maize. "When I told Ian about what we learned from the Abbe Museum curator about the box and collar, he asked Cecil to visit with me. I brought the photos to show him."

"I never thought of Cecil!" exclaimed Gwen. "Leave it to our mayor to know the best local resource for you." Inside, to the immediate left of the door, a small but gracious sitting room gave residents a more formal place to meet various professional people or wait for taxi pickups close to the door.

Annie saw that the room was empty and was pleased that Cecil apparently had chosen a less formal place for them to become acquainted. "So do you know Cecil? What's he like?"

"I don't know him very well. He's been here about five years; he's very quiet for the most part." Gwen paused, glanced around, and continued with a lower voice. "John calls him 'a strange old bird,' but he's always been pleasant to me."

A petite woman with jet-black hair hurried up to Gwen. "I'm so glad you're here early. Can you help me finish up the packets? The copier gave me fits this morning."

"Of course I can, Nora." Gwen turned to Annie. "The receptionist should be able to tell you where to find Cecil. I hope he can give you insight into the mystery. See you soon!" Gwen followed Nora down the main hall. "Nora, are the name tags and markers set out yet?" Annie heard Gwen ask as they hurried along, turning left to enter another wing of the building.

At the reception desk Annie was told Cecil was outside on the observation landing. The receptionist pointed her to a side door, leading to a narrow stone path. Annie followed it, thanking herself for wearing sensible shoes. On a foggy or rainy day the path would have been slippery, but on a bright, almost autumn morning it gave her a small thrill of adventure. When she reached about halfway to the observation deck, Annie could see a man sitting on a bench, a walking stick held lightly between his hands. As she came closer she noticed the man's posture, straight with shoulders back, with no hint of stiffness. Annie could picture him as the star of a chiropractor's demonstration video on proper posture. A couple more steps down and Annie could see glimpses of dark shapes dotting a wide ledge close to the water. Harbor seals.

When Annie reached the deck, the man turned his head toward her. "You must be Annie." His Maine accent mixed with a melodious quality. He stood to greet her. Looking up into his dark, peaceful eyes, Annie smiled back.

"And you must be Mr. Lewey. Thank you for sharing your time with me." Annie sat down on the bench.

"Please call me Cecil." The aged man gestured at the harbor seals. "I don't believe they will be offended, and my family generally only visits on evenings and weekends."

"Have you seen any white-furred holluschickie this year?" As soon as it popped out of her mouth, Annie inwardly winced at how silly she must have sounded. But Cecil chuckled in recognition.

"Not this season. Kotick would have a difficult time finding Sea Cow around here. You are a reader of Kipling?"

"When I was a girl visiting here in the summer, my grandfather would read The Jungle Book stories to me. I was particularly fond of the voice Grandpa used for Sea Catch. 'Empty clamshells and dry seaweed!'" Almost four decades later, the joy of the shared stories warmed Annie.

"I have lived in Stony Point for over thirty years. I wonder if I know your grandfather."

"His name was Charles Holden. He passed away several years ago."

"Charlie!" Cecil exclaimed. "Yes, he would be one to read Kipling to his grandchild." He squinted into the bright sunlight as though he was looking back across the years. "I used to help your grandfather sometimes in his veterinary practice. He understood animals better than most."

"I was convinced he knew everything there was to know. My fourth-grade teacher was quite impressed when I informed her what a pinniped was during the first week of school. We didn't have many of those in Brookfield, Texas. Except at the zoo, of course." As a child, Annie had been fascinated with the animals her grandfather had introduced her to on the Maine coast, and the harbor seals with their sweet faces were one of her favorites.

"Your photo always hung in his office. You were wearing a college T-shirt in the last one I remember. He always said he had hoped you would end up in veterinary science."

"I almost did. Then I realized that I preferred observing and learning about animals to cutting them open. So I decided to keep my thread and needlework limited to handcrafts like crochet and knitting."

"Then you are still carrying on a tradition of your family and honoring your grandmother, as well. Charlie was always proud of you."

"And he always communicated that to me as I was growing up. A blessing I want to pass on to my own grandchildren. Which is one reason why I'm searching for the origin of the American Indian things I found in Gram and Grandpa's attic. If there's a piece of our family's heritage I've missed, I want to fill it in. But I cannot imagine either of my grandparents keeping hidden any part of our heritage."

"I spent many hours swapping stories with Charlie as we attended mares or cattle in labor. I am sure there is no actual Passamaquoddy blood in your family. But in spirit I will always call Charlie Holden my brother."

Annie opened her purse, took the packet of photos from a side pocket and handed them to Cecil. "Do you recognize either of these things?"

Shading the photos with one hand, Cecil carefully examined first the photos of the box and then the regalia collar. "I am sorry to say I have not seen these before. It is clear they were both made by masters. The birch-bark box has many characteristics of those created by Tomah Joseph."

"I saw some of his pieces at the Abbe Museum. I thought I noticed a similarity. But I know so little," said Annie.

"Tomah was the first to sign and date his pieces, or sometimes he would etch 'mikwid hamid' on them."

"What does that mean?"

"Roughly it translates to 'remember me.'"

Annie gazed out over the water, wondering how she could possibly communicate her thoughts after all she had learned the day before. She said simply, "Volumes ring from just two words."

"Yes." Cecil also paused before continuing, examining the photo of the box again. "It looks as though this box was unsigned. It could still be a work of Tomah's or possibly the elder who taught him. It is the work of a Passamaquoddy."

"And the collar?"

"I have not seen this particular combination of colors and pattern. It also looks quite old. Was the fabric used for the base faded?"

"A little, yes."

"I grew up on the reservation at Pleasant Point. We were

not a large tribe by then, and I knew most of the families and the look of their regalia. It was and is an important part of our life. But many people did not stay on the Pleasant Point Reservation, or they lived in Indian Township. The creator may have lived anywhere. How these came to be in your grandparents' attic … well, Keluwosit himself may need to send us the answer." Annie knew from her time at the library that Keluwosit was the Great Spirit and Creator of the Passamaquoddy tradition. She smiled and nodded at Cecil's words.

"Oh." Annie remembered the poem and gave Cecil the printed copy of it. "I also found part of a poem inside the box. I wrote out another copy because the paper was fragile. Here's a photo of the script. I couldn't find any citing of the lines on the Internet or at the library."

Annie watched the seals as Cecil examined the handwriting and the lines. She had missed the nursery period for new pups by a few weeks, but some seals were still molting and "hauled out" onto beaches and ledges during the process.

Cecil raised his head and handed her the photo. "The handwriting looks like the writer could have been taught at a reservation school. The teachers often went to great lengths to anglicize their students. Developing what they called 'a fine hand' was part of that."

"Do you think it's a private poem?"

"That would be my guess, yes. The heart of a woman with one foot each in two different worlds formed this poem. It is what I hear."

Annie nodded again, taking the poem Cecil held out to her and tucking it away in her purse. "It doesn't sound to me like she was forced out of her first world, but that she chose to leave for love. What more can I do to discover where these things came from?"

"Outside of my family, I know of no other registered Passamaquoddy tribe member in Stony Point. But perhaps you could post a description of the collar and box on a genealogy website. I have known people to find parts of their family they didn't know they had lost."

"That's an excellent idea, Cecil! I'll do that this week." From the direction of the Ocean View main building came the clanging of a heavy bell.

"Lunchtime has come rapidly today, thanks to Charlie Holden's granddaughter." Cecil grinned as he stood and extended his right arm to Annie. "May I escort you up the path?"

Annie took his arm. "I'd be delighted. What a wonderful day to meet one of Gram's and Grandpa's friends." She wondered if Ian had known the connection between Cecil and her grandparents. Not one to believe in chance, she decided to simply be thankful for the gift.

"Now that you have, may our paths merge more often." Cecil moved up the stone walk easily, using the walking stick to test the pathway ahead of them.

"I would enjoy that, Cecil. It's not easy these days to find a fellow reader of Kipling."

After walking Cecil to the dining room, Annie drove back toward Grey Gables, letting the morning's experience sink into her. On her drive to Ocean View, she had hoped for either an answer to the origin of the box and collar, or direction on which way to go next. As she left Ocean View behind, she knew she actually had obtained much more. Yes, Cecil's suggestion about a genealogy website would be her next step, and Annie was excited to be tossing out a wider net. Of far more worth was the discovery of Cecil himself and his friendship with Grandpa and Gram. Many people of Stony Point had shared stories and remembrances of Betsy Holden and her gentle touch of grace. Annie loved Grandpa just as deeply, and the stories of Charlie Holden had been more rare. She craved more. Cecil was a memory keeper too, she was convinced, and she looked forward to learning more about him, his family, and his friendship with her grandfather.

Her pondering fueled her trip home. As she came to the long driveway of Grey Gables, she knew she had to share what she had learned that morning with Alice. She pulled the Malibu behind Alice's Mustang, which was parked in front of the carriage house. The windows of the charming, small building were open, and, as Annie came closer to it, she could hear both U2's "Vertigo" and the sounds of movement near the window to the right of the door. If Alice didn't hear her knock on the door, she figured she'd just tiptoe through the flowers and shout through the window.

After thirty seconds of banging, the music lowered. Then the door opened to reveal Alice cradling her caulk gun. Annie put her hands on the top of her head. "I am unarmed, and I come in peace!"

Alice patted the gun like it was a favorite puppy. "Got any leaks? I'll come fix 'em for you. I'm getting the hang of this baby."

"You remind me of the old Rosie the Riveter posters. Would Rosie be interested in some pasta salad for lunch? It's waiting in the fridge."

"Rosie will be over as soon as she gets the caulk out from under her nails." Alice laid the caulk gun down on the seat of the hall tree. At least I got more into the cracks of the windows than I did on myself—I think!"

"After lunch, would you be up for a trip to A Stitch in Time? I want to give myself plenty of time for the project."

"If you'll help me decide what I'm going to make, I would. I have some ideas, but I need to pick one and run with it." Alice took the ball cap off her head, shaking her hair free. "I'll be over in thirty minutes."

"That will give me time to pick some fresh basil to add to the salad. See you soon!"

9

"Fresh basil in pasta salad is heavenly," Alice declared after taking her first bite.

"I hope I can keep the herbs growing in the kitchen as it gets colder," said Annie. "There's just no substitute for fresh." Annie gently tossed her salad to more evenly distribute the basil she had added. "I can hardly believe autumn is right on the doorstep. The twins started kindergarten this week! Of course, the school year usually starts a little earlier in the South."

"Harvest on the Harbor is going to be here before we know it, and I'm still undecided on my project." Alice snagged a piece of rotini and some green pepper on her fork and popped them into her mouth.

"I'm thinking about using Tunisian crochet this time," Annie mused. "It creates this cool reversible effect. But I'm not sure what to make or how to incorporate an American Indian design."

"I keep thinking of the quillwork. That basket with the quillwork rose was gorgeous, and I'd love to do that, but I think embroidery would do it more justice, and I'm not an expert embroiderer, by any standards." Alice paused to sip her water. "There was a design on a birch-bark lid with leaves and a double geometric shape that looked almost like the frame of a lyre. It was so striking! But designing the shape and getting it precise enough would be tough in cross-stitch."

Annie thought back to the day of the museum trip. "Didn't you say something on Tuesday about a chair? Wasn't that quillwork too?"

"That's right! How could I forget? I sketched a pattern for it with a color code while we were at the Abbe. Be right back. Protect my lunch from Boots." Alice left the table to rummage through her purse. She came back with a folded piece of paper. "I'm glad I haven't changed purses this week." Spreading the paper out, she turned it so Annie could see.

"Cross-stitch really does match that design perfectly," Annie said after examining the design. "It would make wonderful place mats, don't you think?"

"The shape would work well, but I'd need to find a backing thick enough to give it substance."

"Mary Beth should have plenty of options to choose from for the right weight and texture. Making the color code was so smart." Annie added a few twists of cracked black pepper to her salad. "Hey, maybe I could do table runners. With the reversible pattern of Tunisian crochet, it would be like getting two table runners in one. What do you think?"

"Both items are sure sellers for harvesttime. People like to do up their tables for the holidays or add accessories like pillows."

"And you should know, Miss Divine Décor."

"Yes, I should. And in my expert opinion, your table-runner idea is the one to run with." Alice almost managed not to smirk at her awful pun. She turned her attention to chasing a black olive around her plate with her fork.

"Would you mind if we stopped at the library before A Stitch in Time?" asked Annie. "Cecil gave me a great suggestion this morning, to post descriptions of the box and regalia collar on some safe genealogy websites."

"Don't mind at all. I have some new catalogs I can drop off for Grace and Josephine. I'll just need to duck into the house to grab them before we leave for town. I want to hear all about your visit with Cecil." Alice scooped up the remaining bits of vegetables on her plate. "I'll drive."

"And I'll let you. Let's get going, I want to have plenty of time to browse around for our supplies and get some tips from Kate, if she's working this afternoon." The friends tidied up the kitchen, made sure to give Boots a little attention, and hurried on their way.

By three thirty, Alice knew all the details of Annie's visit with Cecil and his connection to the Holdens; Grace and Josephine had their new Divine Décor and Princessa catalogs; and Annie had posted her questions on four different genealogy websites after doing a little research to make sure they were safe. Alice and Annie still had plenty of time to explore their options at A Stitch in Time. As they entered their favorite store, Annie was pleased to see Kate behind the counter. She was saying into the phone, "Yes, we do carry square knitting needles. We are open 9 to 6, Monday through Friday and 9 to 4 on Saturday. … You're very welcome." She replaced the handset into its cradle and smiled. "Hi, Alice and Annie. May I help you with anything? Mary Beth is in the office, working on the books."

"We'll have to make sure to say hi to her before we leave. After years of doing the books for our car dealership, I know how lonely it can get back there in the office," said Annie.

"Why do you think I do so much baking? I'm stockpiling comfort foods for when I have to do the paperwork for my business!" Alice grimaced.

"I'm sure Mary Beth will be happy to have a little company by then," Kate agreed. "Have you made your decisions about the Harvest project?"

"We've made some basic plans, but I think we could both use some help with the details," Annie answered. "Alice is farther along in her decisions than I am, so perhaps she should go first. Then she can be gathering up her supplies while you help me narrow things down."

Kate nodded. "All right, Alice. What are you going to make with your wonderful cross-stitch?" She moved from behind the counter.

"I'd like to do place mats using the pattern I saw on the quillwork chair cushions, but I need to figure out what to use for the backing because I don't want them to be too flimsy." Alice handed Kate the pattern she had made.

"Alice, the customers will love this! Let me show you some fabric choices for the backing. What I have in mind will give the mats enough substance but will also wash well." She led Alice over to a wall of display boxes filled with different fabrics for quilters, crafters, and the adventuresome cross-stitcher. "Did you have a color in mind?"

"I want to stick as close to the colors in the panels as I can." Alice pointed toward the middle of her design. "These triangles, as well as this center diamond, are indigo, and I'm thinking an indigo backing would provide contrast for the lighter colors of sage and gold while drawing out those pops of dark blue and also the red." She glanced at Kate's face, gauging her reaction.

"I absolutely agree with you there, Alice." Kate ran her eyes over the bolts of fabric and then pulled one from the mix, turning it to unwrap a section. "How does this one feel to you?"

Alice rubbed the fabric between her thumb and index finger, and then spread the fabric over her hand. "I think this is it. Cut enough for twenty-four place mats."

"You're ambitious!" Kate exclaimed as she took the fabric over to the cutting table. She flipped the bolt until she had unwrapped the needed length and took up the large fabric sheers for the cutting.

"Or crazy," said Alice. "But I have a lot of demonstrations during the month, and cross-stitching is how I relax after them. A cup of tea, a DVD or music, and cross-stitch."

"Mary Beth will be very appreciative of the results of all your relaxation." Kate smiled as she folded the cut fabric. "I can't wait to see all the different contributions on display."

"I know I'm looking forward to seeing *your* contribution," said Alice. From behind a rack of pattern books Annie's voice chimed. "I second that! What are you making, Kate?"

"You two really know how to stroke a woman's ego. I'm making a shawl with a tree pattern that uses positive and negative space to create both the tree and a reflection. The color I'll leave as a surprise."

"Which means we can be sure it won't be green," guessed Alice.

"You'll just have to wait and see." Kate neatly folded the indigo fabric, printed out the yardage and per-unit price, and pinned it to the fabric. "You have plenty to keep you busy while you're waiting to see it."

"My inspiration now has a plan, thanks to you and Annie. Now it's her turn, and I'll go pick out my floss and aida cloth. I get the same rush pulling my colors that I do deciding on a flavor of ice cream at Tanner's Dairy." Alice rubbed her hands together like a child filled with anticipation.

"And you can pick as many as you want without worrying about their glycemic index," said Kate.

"Their *what*?" Alice raised an eyebrow. "Never mind. I don't want to know. I'm having too much fun, and color is calling." She hurried over to the floss display and was soon deep in concentration.

"Annie, what ideas have you gathered so far?" Kate set Alice's fabric on the counter next to the register.

"Well, I'm warning you, my inspiration is much less focused than Alice's," Annie confessed. "I've been a little preoccupied. At Abbe Museum, I tried to take in information for both the project and the mystery. The result is mishmash soup on the brain. But I've been thinking about using Tunisian crochet. It's been a while since I used that method, and I enjoyed the process."

"In the hands of someone with your experience, a Tunisian piece is sure to be an interesting addition to the project," said Kate. "So are you thinking of doing a piece where the reversibility would be highlighted?"

"When Alice and I were talking about it over lunch, I was thinking of making table runners. It would be like the customer's getting two for the price of one. But I'm not sure what kind of pattern to use for it that would be distinctively

Maine American Indian style."

"Were there any museum displays that caught your eye and could be worked in Tunisian?" asked Kate.

"What *didn't* catch my eye," Annie answered ruefully. "But I'm boggled as to how to recreate most of the patterns in Tunisian." Annie fingered a soft skein of pink bamboo yarn as she thought. "Did you see the sea urchin baskets in the museum gift shop?"

"Yes! Very striking graphic and shape," answered Kate.

"I think I could do that in Tunisian, and the reverse would be so interesting. But I doubt it will translate to a flat piece like a runner, now that I think about it more."

Kate bent to pluck some renegade wool fuzz from a basket display of large knitting needles. "I see your point. The graphic would still be interesting, I think, but the inspiration could be obscured. Have you thought of doing round Tunisian crochet pillows? That might translate better than a totally flat piece."

"Hmmm, no, I hadn't." Annie moved on to another skein, this time a silver, alpaca wool, as she thought. "Do you think if I make two pieces in Tunisian crochet with all the rounds the same, and then use the reverse side for the pillow back, that it will work? I saw urchin baskets using combinations of natural reed with taupe stripes and natural with navy stripes. It would be fun to do some of both."

"I can't think of any reason why that wouldn't work," said Kate. "How about working up a test piece for each color combination, and then if they work, you can buy more. If you need to tweak anything, you can exchange whatever you need. Did you have a yarn in mind?"

"Natural fiber, definitely. Maybe a merino and cotton mix?"

"We have a wonderful forty percent merino and sixty percent linen that will be strong enough to keep the pillow's shape but also be soft to the touch." Kate scanned the rainbow collection of yarns. She pulled out one with the color name "champagne" and handed it to Annie. "How does that feel?"

Annie felt the yarn, picturing herself working with it for the next month. "This feels like a winner. I knew you'd be a great help, Kate. This color even mimics the natural wood stripe of the baskets. Now I only need to pick out the accent colors."

"Is there anything else I can help you with, Annie?" To the casual shopper Kate was the perfect example of stellar customer service, but Annie noticed a slight tinge of something else in her voice. Glancing at her watch, she realized how long she and Alice had taken in their decisions. It was past five o'clock. Annie knew Kate probably had things to do before she went home to Vanessa. She didn't want to hinder her.

"No, Kate. I'll just grab more of this champagne and some French blue and ... it's a tie between the sandalwood and cream, so I'll get some of both for test swatches." Annie stacked the skeins of yarn on the counter and sidled up to Alice, who had just pulled down two different shades of aida cloth to compare. She whispered, "It's getting late. Have you found everything? I'm sure Kate needs to get home soon." Louder she said, "We better finish so we can still surprise Mary Beth. It'll be no fun if she comes out by herself."

"And you know how much I love a good surprise," said Alice. She lifted one of the pieces of cloth to Annie's eye level. "I think this is the one for this project."

Annie looked from the cloth to the floss collection in

Alice's shopping basket. "They both would work beautifully, but I like that one a touch better too."

Alice slid the other cloth back in its place on the display, and carried her basket to the front counter. "Kate, I'm ready for checkout." She placed some cash next to her basket. "We'll be right back." Kate smiled as she watched her friends tiptoe toward the door of the shop's office. She was ringing up the floss when Alice noticed some felted animals grazing on the kid's craft table. Plucking up a sheep in one hand and a cow in the other, she mimed a knocking motion to Annie. Annie rapped four times on the office door.

Mary Beth's chair creaked. "Come in." Annie opened the door a couple inches and then stepped back to give Alice a clear path. The sheep entered the office first, prancing on air and trilling, "How are *ewwwwe*?" The cow trailed behind, "I'm *moooody*."

"How *udderly* ridiculous!" Mary Beth exclaimed, as she removed her reading glasses. "Come in, all four of *ewe*."

Annie rescued the cow from Alice's hand. "These are adorable. I have to round up a few for the twins' Christmas box."

"That can be arranged." Mary Beth swiveled her chair to face a computer. "Give me a few seconds to close out this program before I forget." Several taps and a couple clicks later, Mary Beth reversed her swivel. "OK, another task done. So did Cecil have any new information for you?"

Alice nudged Annie. "I guess we know now that Mary Beth had lunch at the same time our esteemed mayor did."

"And you would be wrong." Mary Beth shook her finger at Alice. "The mayor had breakfast at The Cup & Saucer. Peggy pumped him for information and then served it to me at lunch alongside my burger. Well?"

"Nothing really new, actually, although Cecil did confirm that the items did not belong to him, and that he had never seen them. Also, the collar was definitely for a female, like the curator thought. But he did give me the idea of posting descriptions of the box and collar on some genealogy websites."

Alice chimed in, "Which Annie already did before we came to shop."

"I was a little embarrassed to have someone almost the same age as my grandparents remind me of Internet resources."

Alice placed the sheep on Annie's shoulder, nuzzling it against her ear. "Was it a wild and *woolly* situation?"

"You're so *baaaaaad.*" Annie snatched the sheep out of Alice's hand too, chuckling. "It will be worth a little embarrassment if it produces an answer or helps solve the mystery."

10

Alice maneuvered the Mustang up the driveway, stopping about fifteen feet from the porch. "Don't forget, I'll be over tomorrow after my two shows, probably around four."

Annie climbed out of the low-slung car and pulled the bag of goodies from A Stitch in Time out after her. "I'll be sure to butter up Boots before you come."

"That sounds messy!" Alice laughed and put the car in reverse. Annie waved, and then she climbed the steps to the porch. After her busy day, the cozy wicker chair and ocean sounds beckoned to her. Annie was setting her bag beside the chair when she heard the telephone ringing in the living room. Snatching the bag back into her arms, Annie jabbed the key into the dead-bolt. On the fourth ring she grabbed the handset and gasped, "Hello!"

"Mom! Are you all right?" LeeAnn's voice was filled with concern. "You sound horrible. Do you have a respiratory infection or something?"

"LeeAnn, I'm so glad you called." Annie paused for a deep breath to coax her heart rate back to normal. "I'm perfectly healthy. I had just gotten to the porch when I heard the phone ring. Alice and I were shopping in town this afternoon. She had just dropped me off, and I was about to sit myself down in a porch chair when I heard the phone."

Annie set the shopping bag down next to the sofa and made herself comfortable, leaning against Gram's soft pillows and stretching out her legs.

"That's a relief," said LeeAnn. "Your heroic efforts mean one less voice-mail message for you and less patience needed for me. I didn't want to have to wait to tell you about the twins' first week of kindergarten."

"I've been thinking about John and Joanna all week. Do they like their teachers? Did you go through with your plan to have them try being in separate classes?" Annie and LeeAnn had burned up the phone line over the previous six months as LeeAnn and Herb debated the issue of whether the twins should be in the same classroom or separated. The state of Texas had been the second state to approve legislation giving parents the deciding vote in the classroom placement of twins or other multiples of siblings, and LeeAnn and Herb wanted to use that vote wisely.

"Yes, we did. John and Joanna actually liked the idea; it was what they wanted. They have different friends, different interests, and personalities. I think they're hoping to make new friends who like what they like. Herb and I made sure they knew that if they changed their minds and just could not get comfortable in separate classrooms, we would approach the teachers and administration about making a change."

"After their first week, are they still happy with their choice?"

"They seem to be, Mom. Not one peep about missing each other so far. But they've been so tired at the end of the day, maybe they just don't have the energy!"

Annie smiled at a rising memory. "Like mother, like children. I remember your first week at kindergarten. You talked my ear off from the second you climbed off the bus until I set a snack in front of you. Then you'd fall asleep with your braids dipping into your milk. But you adjusted quickly, and I'm sure John and Joanna will too."

LeeAnn chuckled. "Thank you for not taking a photo of me in that position and enlarging it for my high school graduation party."

"It was tempting, I tell you. You looked so adorable. Where are Joanna and John? Can I say hello to them?"

"I made dinner early since they were so tired. They'll be having their baths soon, but they would love to talk to you." LeeAnn pulled the phone away from her mouth and called out, "Who wants to talk with Grammy?"

Her stomach rumbling, Annie took the opportunity to carry the phone into the kitchen. She could hear the voices of her grandchildren yelling, "Me!" "I do!" Muffled at first and gradually growing louder, Annie could picture their progress through the house to the phone. She filled the teakettle under the faucet and placed it on a back burner. Just as she opened the refrigerator door to hunt for the leftover black bean soup she planned to heat for dinner, she heard Joanna's voice in her ear.

"Hi, Grammy! Did you hear the wish I made last night all the way up there?"

"What did you wish?" Annie pulled a small saucepan from a cabinet and poured the soup into it. The saucepan went on the burner next to the kettle.

"I told Jesus I wished I could tell you all about my new teacher and the kids in my class and the way bigger playground.

And now I can!" Joanna's little voice grew more and more excited until it was punctuated by a stifled yawn.

"That's one of my favorite kinds of wishes." Annie selected a wooden spoon from a bouquet of utensils blooming from a stoneware crock and stirred the soup, adjusting the flame so it would heat slowly. "Tell me all about it."

The next ten minutes were filled with colorful descriptions of the new school building and Mrs. Bop, the teacher, and why Joanna thought Morgan was going to be her newest good friend. Joanna concluded by informing Annie that a magician was going to perform at school the next day, the last day of the first week, and that John kept tugging on her arm so she had to go.

"I loved hearing about your first week of kindergarten, Joanna! And I love you very much. Good night, sweetheart!"

"I love you too, Grammy. I miss you more than a bear misses honey." Joanna passed the phone over to John.

"Grammy, I thought Joanna would never give me a turn! Guess what? My teacher, Mrs. Ensign, asked us to bring in our favorite toy animal tomorrow, and she's going to take our pictures with them to put on the bulletin board."

"What a fun idea, John. Which animal are you taking?"

"The gray whale you gave me, of course! Whales rule."

John's comment reminded Annie of her recent conversation with Ian. "Whales are amazing creatures, for sure. A friend of mine here tells me there is a maritime museum not too far away with all kinds of displays about boats and whales. I'm going to send you a brochure in my next letter."

"Awesome! When can we come? Do you know what kind of boats they have?"

"You're just going to have to come and see for yourself. And make sure you read the brochure with your mom."

"Grammy, send it right now."

"The post office is closed for the night, but I promise to send it tomorrow. How do you like your classmates?"

"I like them so far, 'specially Tyler. He's funny and didn't even get mad when he couldn't eat the cupcakes Sara's mother made for us. He has celery disease."

"That's an illness I don't recognize."

"Tyler's dad talked to us about it. Celery disease is when you can't eat anything made with wheat stuff. It makes Tyler really sick if he eats any."

"Oh, Tyler has celiac disease."

John spoke with a consciously polite tone. "Yes, Grammy, that's what I already told you. Anyway, when Tyler heard I had a twin sister, he gave me his cupcake for Joanna. She liked that a lot."

"How thoughtful of Tyler. Your other classmates didn't mind you getting the extra cupcake?"

"Nah, none of them have a twin. They think that's neat, even though Joanna's a girl, so we can't switch places and play tricks on people."

LeeAnn cut into the conversation. "John, it's bath time. Daddy's waiting for you upstairs. Say goodnight to Grammy."

"I have to go get clean, Grammy. I love you. Don't forget to send the museum thing."

"I won't, John. Tell Daddy I said hello. Love you!"

"Bye." Annie heard his small legs charging up the stairs and his holler. "I have to get my whales, Daddy. They're dirty too."

LeeAnn was back on the line. "They miss you so much, Mom, even though you were here just a couple of weeks ago."

"What more can I do to convince you to come to Maine for Thanksgiving vacation?" Annie asked. "I found a maritime museum that is perfect for John. And the weather will actually be cool enough for a fire! All of you will love Stony Point, I just know it."

"John and Joanna are already doing a good job of convincing me. During nightly prayer they keep asking Jesus if they can go to Maine, and if He'd help them get there. Herb is a little concerned that the travel will be too tiring for the twins, but I think he'll realize they can handle it once they get more used to school and aren't so tired all week."

"I'm joining John and Joanna in their prayers. You know the Bible says that the Lord works and who can hinder it? There's a special surprise I'm cooking up for when you come." Annie couldn't wait any longer. She ladled the soup into a bowl and cut a piece of corn bread. She would tell LeeAnn about the mystery next time when she wasn't so hungry. Maybe she'd have more answers by then from the website posts.

"Stop! You have me wanting to hop on a plane tomorrow, and then Joanna would miss seeing the magician," LeeAnn protested with laughter in her voice. "I need to go, Mom. If I'm not there at bath time, Joanna will leave soap in her hair, and it will look like straw all day tomorrow. We'll talk soon."

"Enjoy your weekend, Honey. Good night!"

"Love you, Mom. Bye!"

Annie clicked the "end call" button and placed the cordless phone on the kitchen table. After taking a quick bite of the corn bread, she carried the plate and bowl from counter to table. She turned back for her tea, sipping the decaf Earl Grey. Boots padded her way down the hall and into the kitchen, stopping for a brief drink at the water bowl.

"I guess I'm not the only thirsty one in the house," said Annie. "Boots, you'll be happy to know I'm staying home tomorrow. It's looking more and more certain that we'll be having company over Thanksgiving. I need to get the baker's rack down from the attic and get everything set up for making the rose-hip jelly. It's almost picking time." Boots swished her tail and twitched her ears before slipping under the table and settling herself on top of Annie's feet. Annie smiled at the thought of having a Boots blanket over the winter months, albeit a blanket with an ornery mind of its own. She turned her attention to the nourishing and delicious meal, replaying her conversation with Joanna and John in her mind. "Thank you, Lord, for keeping us free of celery disease so the twins can experience toast with rose-hip jelly this autumn." Annie allowed herself the laugh she had suppressed during her conversation with John.

After dinner was finished, and the dishes cleaned and put away, Annie settled on the living room couch to begin her first pillow. She laid the copy of the poem fragment and her notes from the museum on the arm of the couch where she could see them for inspiration and guidance. Pulling the skeins of yarn from the bag beside the couch, Annie decided to start with the champagne and French blue colors, and put the sandalwood and cream colors away for later.

Selecting the right-size Tunisian crochet hook from the stash in her tote, Annie began chaining the champagne yarn. When the chain was the right length, she skipped the first chain, inserted the hook in the back horizontal bar of the next chain, wrapped the yarn over the hook, and pulled up a loop. As Annie pulled up loops in each of the chains, she murmured the words of the poem. The first two lines reminded her of a day almost twenty-five years before, when LeeAnn was young enough to be content in a stroller for a day at the zoo. They had wandered along paths lined with habitats for bears, lemurs, big cats, and gibbons until they came upon a miniature river populated with otters. While Annie had, as always, appreciated the power and grace of the black leopards, ocelots, and Sumatran tigers, she couldn't stop watching the river otters as they slipped from the riverbank to dart through the water, and then flipped off the sides to change directions. *Water dancing*, she thought, *just as the writer of the poem had said*. Annie had been entranced by the otters' dance too. She suspected that if she lived in a place where she saw otters often, she would feel a keen kinship with them also.

Annie pulled up the last loop on the hook and then turned her work to begin crocheting with the French blue yarn on the return pass. "Where would you dance?" She would have mourned for the one who was so obviously taken out of her natural element, if not for those four little words. "If love took you" changed everything. Annie had not always loved being the bookkeeper for the car dealership in Texas. While she pursued her studies at Texas A&M, she hadn't been dreaming of a career in bookkeeping. But she did love Wayne, and their lunches together, quick moments of laughter, or even the flash of a smile across the showroom as she came out to refill her coffee mug, infused the hours of balancing, tallying, and recording with meaning. Had the poem's author ever come to the place in her heart where she felt in her element again, even if she was never restored to her natural habitat? Where *had* that natural habitat been? How did Stony Point fit in her life history, if it did at all?

Annie began a forward pass of Tunisian purl stitch with the French blue yarn; she liked the effect of the contrasting colors. Boots entered the cozy room, jumping onto one of the chairs facing the couch. She curled up in a loose ball, tucking her paws into her chest. "Ah, Boots, what am I going to do about this project? The colors are perfect, but I'm not so sure this pillow is going to end up anywhere near doing justice to those gorgeous urchin baskets." Boots turned her eyes toward Annie for a couple of seconds, and then closed them and lowered her head to settle in for a nap.

"It's a good thing Alice is coming over tomorrow. You're no creative help."

11

The early morning sun was slung low over the water, a slash of heavy clouds hovered above it, as though it threatened to keep the sphere from rising any higher. Annie decided she had picked the best time of the day for a quick walk among the beach roses to check how close they were to perfect ripeness. As she gently squeezed a hip, a gust of wind tore at her. The hips were almost ripe for picking, and the day seemed ripe for rain. A good day for working in the house.

"Don't ripen too fast, you rose hips. I still have some setup to accomplish." Annie moved farther down hill, noting she'd have a bumper crop to cook up, if she found Gram's recipe and equipment soon, and if she could harvest the hips before they went mushy. Wind swirled around her again, setting the hardy beach roses swaying side to side like the ladies in the Zumba class at the community center. As Annie hiked back up the hill, she marveled at the strong beauty of beach roses. No hothouse flowers for this hill, tended by a diligent gardener keeping pests at bay. No human caretaker, anyway. And yet the blooms' charm matched those of cherished rare flowers to Annie.

Annie paused at the boot scrape, which had stood beside the back porch steps as long as she could remember, and wiped the bottom of her shoes clean. A horn beeped twice—it was Alice on her way to her first Princessa and Divine Décor parties of the day. Annie put a hand up to wave, but ended up clapping it to the top of her head instead, as yet another blast of wind tried to snatch her cap. *Alice better hold on tight to her samples while she's unloading today!* Annie thought as she darted inside to the kitchen.

After fortifying her resolve with a cup of Irish Breakfast tea, Annie climbed the stairs to the attic with a bucket filled with microfiber cloths and a spray bottle of wood cleaner dangling from her arm. As she stood in the doorway of the attic, the clouds scuttling across the sun gave a strobe effect to the dim light coming in through the window. "Thank you, Grandpa, for wiring the attic for electricity when you bought Grey Gables," Annie whispered, pulling the string on the ceiling light fixture.

She wove through the stacks to the baker's rack, realizing she would need to clear a wider pathway to the door, or she'd never be able to maneuver the rack anywhere near it. But the first thing to be cleared was the rack itself.

Annie set the bucket and spray down on the floor next to the rack. Wanting to avoid any flying objects this time, she looked around for something to climb on to ensure the top of the rack was completely empty. She spied a sturdy-looking bench pushed up under an old vanity and slid it over to the rack. Resting her right knee on top of the bench, Annie leaned her weight onto the bench to see if it was as sturdy as it looked. There were no groaning or splintering sounds, so she grabbed a couple of cloths and the spray bottle and climbed up on the bench. There was nothing there but enough dust to stuff a duvet. One cloth was sacrificed in collecting the majority of the dust. Annie sprayed the other with the wood cleaner and wiped away the remaining dust and grime, leaving behind the pleasant smell of cedar wood and bergamot essential oils. Stepping down off the bench, she dragged it back to the vanity table and moved on to the next shelf.

A solid wood crate occupied the left side of the shelf. Annie tested its weight by grasping it by the wood trim and lifting it up a couple of inches. The crate proved lighter than she expected for its size and was easily moved. Lowering it to the floor, Annie removed the lid to find a garland of red, white, and blue fabric. Pulling a couple of handfuls of the garland from the crate, Annie saw rosettes were attached about every four feet. She had seen this garland every Independence Day during her childhood, when her grandparents celebrated the blessings of America's freedom by festooning Grey Gables's expansive porch. She wished she had found it earlier in the summer to carry on the tradition, but she was determined to find a place for the crate where she would be able to locate it the next summer. For the time being, Annie slid it under the vanity bench.

The next occupant to be relocated from the baker's rack was a bushel basket bearing the stamp of Bailey's Orchard, Whitefield, Maine. It bristled with gardening stakes and plant markers labeled in Betsy's handwriting—basil, thyme, sage, oregano, lavender, zucchini, green peppers, and such. Annie carefully removed the basket from the shelf and set it to the right of the vanity, hoping she'd remember to use them next planting season.

"Two shelves down, two to go." On the third shelf, a dark gray, open-blade fan stood atop a rectangular cardboard box, sitting a few degrees to the left. Annie saw that the base of the fan extended across a ridge made by the flaps of the box, having been alternated and tucked in rather than taped. She moved the metal fan to the top of the vanity where it stood as straight as a West Point cadet during inspection. Inserting several fingers into the tucked flaps of the box, Annie pulled up and let out a soft "Yes!" of triumph when she realized what was inside. Betsy's canning jars, the very size she and Annie used for the rose-hip jelly. Not one jar was missing a ring or lid. Tucking the flaps closed once again, Annie carried the box and set it next to the attic door to bring down to the kitchen when she was done. Heightened curiosity spurred her on to the next item, a round tin the color of dairy cream with brown speckles. The words "Charles Chips" in the same cream color stood out against a splotch of dark brown. Many a childhood summer evening was spent on the porch listening to the waves, sharing stories, and passing the speckled tin of potato chips between them—Gram, Grandpa, and Annie.

Annie pried off the lid, delighted to find Gram's jelly bags nesting there. Used for draining the juice from the boiled rose hips, frugal canners used all sorts of things to make their own bags. Some used old stockings, worn pillowcases or even cloth diapers, but Gram had sewn her own from muslin. Annie pulled out three folded bags, each bottom section a faint orangey pink from the juice, before reaching in to feel a different kind of fabric. Much thicker than the jelly-bag muslin, the folds fell open as Annie lifted it free from the tin. It was a child-sized apron, the one Betsy had made for Annie when she was six years old. When she had first put it on, the hem fell to below her knees, and the ties made giant bows as they drew the sides of the apron to almost meet in the back. No matter what kind of mess Annie made, the clothes beneath remained pristine. Each summer that followed, the apron's length was a bit shorter and the back bows a little smaller. Gram's foresight had given Annie an apron she had used until adolescence hit, and her last growth spurt had finally forced her to exchange the special apron for a larger one.

Annie spread the apron out on the shelf, looking for tears or worn areas. The cheery fabric was a touch faded, but the seams were strong with no broken threads. Gram had sewn it with her usual meticulousness, and Annie had no doubt Joanna would be able to wear it for several years, just as she had. Refolding the apron, she placed it, and the jelly bags, back into the tin and set the tin on top of the box of jelly jars. She removed the final item from the third shelf, a box of miscellaneous old linens and doilies, and slid it on top of the bench. Only one shelf remained to be cleared, and Annie didn't waste any time digging into the boxes that lined the bottom of the rack. Two boxes—one wide and squat, and one tall and narrow—contained various instruments and supplies from her grandfather's veterinary practice. As Annie carried them over to pile in a wedge of space near the vanity, she wondered if Cecil had held any of the things as he helped Grandpa with the animals around the Stony Point area.

The last two boxes, containing the jelly-bag tripod Grandpa had rigged for Gram and quart-size canning jars, joined the collection by the door to be carried downstairs.

Only one thing remained to be found before Annie could start picking the rose hips—Gram's recipe. Annie finished cleaning each of the rack's shelves and stepped back to admire her work. Free of decades-old dust and grime, the oak's warm tone would look cozy and inviting against the jersey cream color of the kitchen walls.

Her last task of the morning was to clear the path for the rack to be moved downstairs when Alice came later to help. The solid piece of furniture was heavy enough without it catching on a box or dragging a bench along with it. By the time Annie had shifted the piles of miscellany to one side of the attic space or the other, her muscles were ready for a break. Sliding the bucket over her left arm, she curled her right arm around the Charles Chips tin to carry it down to the kitchen. The pasta salad had been calling her for the past hour, and Annie's throat was parched.

A squall dashed rain at a slant against the windows of the house. When she reached the bottom of the stairs, Annie saw Boots curled up, napping on the couch, and she felt like curling up next to her. But she went to the kitchen instead and dipped up a bowl of pasta salad and poured a giant glass of cool water, adding a long squeeze of lemon. The simple meal didn't take long to finish, but its effect was almost immediate. Annie decided, rather than napping, to use her renewed energy to work on the pillow until Alice arrived. She settled down on the unoccupied end of the couch and lost herself in the steady rhythm of champagne Tunisian knit stitch and French blue Tunisian purl stitch. After several rows, Annie fastened off the French blue, completed a forward pass with champagne, turned it, and began working with the cream yarn for the return pass. "Hmmmm, nice," Annie nodded to herself. "But will it reflect the urchin basket design? I just can't tell." Boots opened one eye, as though about to weigh in with her opinion, only to shut it again.

As the afternoon wore on, the rain wore out. By the time Alice came knocking at the door the water was dripping from the eaves sporadically.

"Wouldn't you know it, the rain stops as soon as I make it home and change into comfortable clothes," Alice said as she stepped into the hall.

"Terrible weather for heels." Annie took Alice's anorak to hang it on the coatrack. "Did any of your profits blow away with the wind?"

"Thankfully, the profits stayed put and made the messiness all worthwhile. My hostesses were thrilled. I think they'll be regulars." Alice combed her fingers through her hair. "So while I'm in a good mood, tell me what we're tackling tonight."

"I spent the morning cleaning the baker's rack in the attic and clearing a path to the door. The first thing I want us to do is carry it down to the kitchen. You'll be happy to know I found the canning jars, jelly bags, and the tripod all stored on the rack—almost everything I need for jelly making."

"Have you found Betsy's recipe yet?" asked Alice, as they started up the stairs.

"Not yet, but I'm hopeful after finding the other things. If the rose hips get to the point where they're almost past their peak, and if I still haven't found the recipe, I'll look up a recipe online. Then I'll have a whole year to find Gram's."

"With the intimate relationship I maintained over the years with Betsy's rose-hip jelly, I'm hoping it won't come to that," Alice said.

"I will make it my mission to reunite the two of you before the season is over," Annie said as she opened the attic door.

"Whoa! I wasn't the only woman working hard this morning." Alice punctuated her approval with a low whistle. "I've never seen this much of the attic floor boards in my life."

"At least I didn't have to wear heels all day like you. For that difficult feat, I'll let you have the forward-facing end of this chore." Annie plucked an old tablecloth from a box of old linens, rolled it into a tube, and bent to wedge it under the attic door to keep it from closing.

"If you insist." Alice placed herself at the left side of the rack, trying different holding positions for the easiest lifting. She bent her knees and grabbed the vertical posts under the second shelf from the bottom. "I'm ready when you are."

Annie moved into position. "OK, lift!" Both women raised their side of the rack, Annie glancing behind her to make sure they were not veering away from the clear path. She shuffled backward at a steady pace so she wouldn't jerk the rack out of Alice's grip. When they reached the door, Annie gasped, "Set it down for a minute."

"That's one wicked solid piece of furniture!" Alice exclaimed. "It could stand up in any nor'easter."

"Good thing too, since I have two sou'westers named Joanna and John heading our way." Annie paused to access the best way to maneuver the rack down the two flights of stairs. "Let's turn the rack horizontal." Annie stepped through the doorway and down one step.

"Are you ready for me to tilt it toward you?" Alice asked, bending to look at Annie between the shelves.

"Tilt away." Annie raised her hands to grab the top of the rack as soon as it was close enough. They descended cautiously, reaching the landing of the second floor without a problem. After catching their breath and shaking out their arms for a moment, Annie and Alice hefted the piece again for the trip down the main staircase. The generous foyer on the first floor gave them ample space to bring the rack easily around the corner for the trip down the hallway to the kitchen. Once they had the rack positioned in its former spot, Annie and Alice collapsed onto kitchen chairs.

Alice looked around the kitchen at the updates Annie had made since she inherited Grey Gables from Betsy. "The baker's rack is exactly what was missing. There's a perfect balance between new and old now."

"I think so too," said Annie. "And just picture a shelf or two filled with jars of Gram's jelly." Annie snapped two fingers. "Oh, almost forgot! I put together a meatloaf this morning for our dinner." She left her chair to set the oven to preheat. Before returning to the table, she put the kettle on for tea and served up two slices of corn bread.

"This is a meatloaf kind of day, if ever there was one," said Alice, "and a snack kind of afternoon too. I never eat enough on a double- or triple-booked day. Bring on the corn bread and don't forget the honey bear!"

The two friends enjoyed their tea and bread before diving into the charming mess that was the library.

12

"My goal for the library is to arrange everything so John and Joanna can reach books and things that might interest them. And are appropriate, of course." Annie and Alice stood facing a wall of built-ins crammed with reading material. Over the years, what had begun as an organized collection had been multiplied, shifted, separated, and put back together so many times it resembled a reading jungle. Determined not to be overwhelmed by the size of the goal, Annie had narrowed her focus. "Let's begin by going shelf by shelf and pulling anything the kids might like. We'll tackle the desk another time."

Alice turned to scan the other side of the room, lined with identical stuffed built-ins. "Do you still have the step stool that used to be in here? We're going to need it."

"It's in the family room, very handy for dusting the moldings." Annie went to fetch the stool as Alice began removing books from a few of the lower shelves, stacking them next to a leather reading chair. Annie returned with the white metal, three-step stool and placed it in front of the first stack of shelves. "I'll climb up and look through the books. When I hand one to you, dust it and give it a place on a lower shelf." Annie climbed up to the highest step.

"Do you want me to separate fiction books from

nonfiction?" Alice asked as she wiped the dust from the shelves she had just emptied.

"Yes! John loves looking at the pictures in encyclopedias, field guides, and other nonfiction books about animals, boats, oceans, you name it. Having them all in one low section will be really helpful." Annie ran her eyes along the top shelf, while she ran a lamb's-wool wand along the tops and spines of the books. "Nothing suitable on this shelf." On the next highest shelf Annie found some nonfiction animal books and a couple of classics—*Heidi* and *Mr. Popper's Penguins*—and handed them down to Alice. Once they were in a rhythm of scan, pull, dust, and reshelve, Annie asked Alice, "Did you have a chance to start your place mats?"

"I only had a little time last night after I had everything packed for the shows today." Alice reached up for the book Annie was dangling down toward her, *Birds of the Eastern United States*.

"How is the pattern looking in the actual stitches? Does it look like you thought it would?" Annie stretched over to snag a book at the end of the row, a collection of Beatrix Potter stories. "Of course, I'm asking because I'm the one who's not so confident about her project."

"I've only done one side of the border, so it's probably too early to know how it's going to look when it's completed. My main concern isn't if the pattern will look nice, because the colors are looking beautiful together already." Alice settled the dust-free story collection on its new shelf. "But what if I copied the pattern wrong, and it comes out looking unlike any Micmac pattern ever used? I would hate that."

"Exactly! I don't want to put something in the Harvest

sale that's as off-kilter as a three-legged armadillo."

A muffled snort escaped Alice. "First of all, no self-respecting armadillo would be caught dead—three-legged or not—up here in Maine! Secondly, I don't think anything you make will be that off!" She dusted a book about clipper ships and slipped it onto the nonfiction side of the shelf. "Hmmm, I wonder if any of the others are second-guessing themselves as much as we are. How about I give everyone a quick call and ask?"

Annie stepped down off the stool. "Good, you can do that while I check on the meatloaf and put the stewed tomatoes and green beans on to cook." Alice followed her into the kitchen and retrieved her cell phone from her purse. She had entered all the Hook and Needle Club members into her speed-dial list. Annie followed the one-sided conversations, surprised at the evidence that almost all the members were having doubts about their pieces, even Kate.

Alice's phone shut with a soft click. "Congratulations, we're normal! What do you think about an emergency meeting tomorrow during Peggy's afternoon break? Together, maybe we can figure out a solution so we can all finish our pieces by the Harvest on the Harbor celebration."

"Let's do it. We don't have any time to lose." Annie lowered the flame under the tomatoes. "The green beans need a few more minutes; you have time to confirm the meeting with everyone. Just tell Mary Beth and Peggy to pass it on, and everyone will be there, two thirty sharp."

After a dinner fit for two hard-working women, Annie and Alice returned to the library. By the end of the evening they had pulled all the appropriate books for the twins from upper shelves, and there was already a nice-size collection in the dedicated section Alice had cleared. Exhausted and pleased with what they had accomplished, Annie walked Alice to the front door.

"I could go home and chug two liters of Mountain Dew and still fall asleep as soon as I crawl into bed," Alice said as she pulled on her anorak. "Only one Princessa/Divine Décor party after the meeting tomorrow, so I can sleep in late!"

Annie followed Alice out onto the porch. "You earned every extra minute, my friend. Thanks for your help."

"No sweat. Figuratively speaking, that is." Alice started down the steps. "See you tomorrow!"

Annie watched Alice as she made her way to the carriage house. She rubbed her bare arms as the crisp evening air chilled her. The moment Alice disappeared behind her door, Annie slipped back inside. Boots was sitting on the bottom step, staring at the door, when Annie entered the foyer.

"Come upstairs, Boots," said Annie as she stepped past the cat on the way to her bedroom. "I could use a foot warmer tonight."

****

By the time Peggy bustled through the door of A Stitch in Time at two thirty-five, the other members, except for Mary Beth, were settled in their seats. "I'm sorry, but I can't stay long," she gasped to her friends. "Lisa has a horrible cold, and we don't want her sneezing all over the customers." She dropped into a seat next to Gwendolyn, who patted her on the shoulder.

"I'm sorry to hear Lisa isn't feeling well. We'll try to

be as efficient as we can," Gwen reassured her. The other members nodded or murmured agreement.

"I'll sum up why we called the meeting," said Alice. "Annie and I were talking about how we aren't feeling very confident about our patterns, now that we've started them. We wondered if anyone else was feeling the same, and after some calls we found out almost everyone was! So what can we do to fix the problem?"

Mary Beth hurried over to the group. "Sorry about that. One of our suppliers is having computer problems and lost our order. What exactly is the source of the doubts? Have you designed your projects to be too hard to execute? With the level of technical skills this group possesses that would surprise me."

"I'll share first, if you don't mind," said Peggy. "I could get called back to the diner any second." She glanced around the circle, seeing only encouraging faces. "The pattern I decided to use has a red background with cattails and stars in gold. You probably remember how much I liked those colors on the museum flag. There was a birch-bark picture frame that had cattails, stars, and one of those—what did they call it?—oh yeah, a double geometric shape. Well, I just wanted to use the cattails and stars because I couldn't make the geometric pattern look good enough. But then I started thinking, what if there's a particular reason for the three things to be together on the frame? A lot of the pieces at the museum had the geometric shape, so is it OK to leave that out?"

"Peggy, I think your concern about making changes in patterns is natural," said Kate. "We all want to create pieces that reflect the spirit of the American Indian people, that show what was and is important to them. That's hard to do when you don't speak their language, in a sense, or share their history. I know from the museum exhibits how important trees are to the Abenaki culture, but what I don't know is whether the pattern I'm using to create my tree shawl reflects that importance in a recognizable way. Does that make sense?"

"Kind of like how Chinese food in America isn't much like Chinese food in China?" Alice suggested.

"I'd say that's an accurate analogy," said Gwen. "It captures my concerns about my project, as well. In the same way that we don't want to give people a false depiction of Stony Point as a community, I don't want to assume my piece is saying 'Maine American Indian' if it's actually saying 'cheap knockoff made in Taiwan.'"

"We want to honor the tribes, not insult them," inserted Annie. Heads nodded around the circle.

"I have a suggestion," said Stella after silently listening to the ladies' concerns. "Would each of you be willing to put your designs down on paper, including both the pattern and the colors you plan to use? I would be glad to return to the Abbe Museum with the designs and consult privately with one of the curators." She glanced down at her watch. "If we call right now, we may be able to schedule something for early next week. The museum is open on Saturday."

"Kezi was wonderfully helpful," said Annie. "She knew so much about the way designs have changed through the years and American Indian art as it relates to their history. If she's available, I'd recommend her."

"Stella, I'd be glad to go with you," Gwen volunteered. "My schedule for Monday is very flexible, if that's not too soon for the curators."

Mary Beth gestured toward the door to the shop's office. "Stella, why don't you use the office phone and call right now." Stella stepped into the office, closing the door behind her. The women talked among themselves for only a few minutes before Stella reappeared.

"Kezi was pleased to hear about our request and will meet with Gwen and me at two thirty on Monday," reported Stella. "If everyone brings their designs to Mary Beth by ten o'clock on Monday morning, Gwen and I will show them all to Kezi and write down any comments or suggestions she has."

"Stella—and Gwen, too, of course—thank you for being our ambassadors," said Mary Beth. "Alice and Annie, thank you for bringing up your concerns. I truly do think this will end up being our most interesting Harvest on the Harbor sale yet. I think we can call this meeting adjourned."

"And I call myself gone," said Peggy. "Back to the diner for me. Bye, everyone!" She waved her manicured fingers at her friends and swept out the door.

"I'm off to party," said Alice. "Divine Décor party, that is." She lifted a plastic bag to show Annie. "Have heels, will party."

"Better you than me." Annie laughed. "You've obviously recuperated from last night."

"I'm not even going to tell you what time I rolled out of bed this morning."

"I should have sent Boots home with you. She woke me up at sunrise, the stinker." Annie waited for Alice as she exchanged her comfortable flats for heels and then walked with her toward the door. The two friends parted on the sidewalk, one to work in someone else's home and one to work in her own.

Before Annie reached her Malibu she heard her name being called. Turning around, she saw Ian across the street waiting for a car to pass. His schnauzer Tartan stood leashed beside him. "Hi, Ian! Hi, Tartan!" The street clear again, the two trotted over to her.

"Are you enjoying your Saturday, Annie?" Ian asked.

"Yes, I am." Annie gave Tartan a soft scratch around the top of his head and under his chin. Standard size for his breed, Tartan was no shorty. He stepped closer to Annie and nudged her for more attention, almost knocking her off balance.

"Hey, watch it, buddy." Ian tightened the slack of the leash a bit. "I'm sorry; it's clear he hasn't been getting enough attention with all the evening budget meetings this week. We're going to have a nice long romp on the beach this afternoon."

"It sounds like both of you will enjoy stretching your legs." Annie smiled. "Even public servants need a romp once in a while, I think. Maybe even more than most folks."

"You could be right. We should put it on the official agenda. Don't be surprised if you see the whole budget committee strolling along the beach some day." Ian smiled down into Annie's eyes. "Hey, how did your visit with Cecil go?"

"It was wonderful. When you suggested I talk with Cecil, did you know he was friends with my grandparents?"

Ian thought for a moment, running his hand over Tartan's wiry coat. "The day I suggested you visit Cecil, I was just thinking about Cecil's heritage, and how easy it always is to talk with him. But now that you mention it, I do remember taking our family dog to Dr. Holden when I was a teenager, and Cecil was assisting in the office that day. I'd totally forgotten about that."

"Well, it was a few years ago." Annie grinned. "And you're right, Cecil is very easy to talk with. Though he didn't recognize the things from the attic, he confirmed what I learned at the Abbe Museum and gave me a suggestion that I'm hoping will bring us closer to solving this mystery. We're going to visit again, and I'm looking forward to hearing more about his friendship with Grandpa and Gram."

"That's the kind of results we public servants like to hear." Ian reined Tartan in as the dog started to wander too close to the street. "And friends like it even more. I'm thankful Todd reacquainted me with Cecil several years ago, or I would not have remembered to suggest him to you. And I would have lost out on many excellent conversations as well." He took a quick step forward, off balance, as Tartan suddenly lunged at a bird that lighted on the back of a bench. "Whoa, boy!"

"Looks like Tartan *really* needs that romp." Annie chuckled. "Thanks again for your help, Ian."

"It's my pleasure, Annie," said Ian. "Let me know if Cecil's suggestion brings anything interesting into the mix."

"I will." Annie reached over to give Tartan a quick pat before parting. "Enjoy your romp!"

She watched the two as they moved along the sidewalk toward the beach. They almost made her want to add a dog to her household. *Wouldn't Boots just love that!* Annie thought as she opened the door of her car to head home and put her sea urchin design down on paper.

13

The members of the Hook and Needle Club all met at A Stitch in Time to deliver their designs before ten o'clock, except for Peggy who was busy with the late breakfast crowd at The Cup & Saucer. She had given her design to Mary Beth much earlier when she had served up Mary Beth's omelet, telling her, "I wish I was as good at designing quilts as Wally is at making those toy boats."

"I think you—like your husband—are underestimating your skills, Peggy," Mary Beth reassured her. "If there is anything that needs tweaking, you'll know tomorrow." Peggy had given a quick nod and hurried off to another table.

Annie and Alice drove into town separately since Alice had to leave immediately after the meeting for a Divine Décor regional sales meeting in Portland. Annie had firmly reminded herself not to linger long. She hoped she would find Gram's jelly recipe among the rest of the piles and shelves awaiting her at home in the library. And it needed to be found soon; rose hips wait for no woman. As they chatted with Mary Beth and Kate, Gwen breezed through the door with a cheerful smile for them all and with a leather portfolio in which to transport the designs to the museum in style.

Mary Beth added Peggy's design to those of Kate, Annie, and Alice, and handed them to Gwen, who neatly inserted them into the portfolio. After glancing at her watch,

Alice said, "If Jason doesn't drive up in the next minute or two, I think the tide is going to reverse itself." The chuckles amped up a notch when a long shadow moved in front of the door and stopped. Stella had arrived. They watched out of the corner of their eyes as Jason walked around from the driver's side of the old Lincoln to open the passenger door for their friend. Stella spoke to her longtime chauffer and friend, but the women could not make out her words. She paused to straighten the collar of Jason's jacket before leaving him behind on the sidewalk to enter the store.

"I apologize for my lateness," Stella said as soon as the door had closed behind her. Though she was technically not late at all, Stella held to the axiom: "To be on time is to be late; to be early is to be on time." Her friends knew better than to argue the point with her. "Jason had not yet checked the Lincoln's tires this week, and that just wouldn't do with us driving to Bar Harbor today. Therefore, we needed to first stop at the GasNGo."

"Your foresight is very much appreciated, Stella," said Gwen. She lifted the portfolio to show her longtime friend. "I have all the designs, so I'm ready to leave when you are."

"Please send Kezi my regards," said Annie. "Oh, I almost forgot." She showed the ladies a canvas tote with a zipped cover. "Kezi asked me to bring in the box and collar. Would you mind showing them to her when you meet with her?" Annie knew the fragile items would be in capable hands.

Stella held out a hand to take the tote. "Of course."

"Thank you both," said Annie. "I'm so excited to hear the comments tomorrow at the meeting!" Mary Beth, Kate and Alice chimed in with their thanks as Gwen and Stella made their way to the door. They watched Jason open the door for Stella again—a rear door this time—and then Gwen. With his passengers settled, Jason turned to smile and wave to the ladies in the store before sliding in behind the wheel.

When the Lincoln had driven out of sight down Main Street, the other members of the club shook themselves out of their thoughts and hurried along to their individual commitments. Annie returned to Grey Gables, where she opened windows to invite the gentle breeze in to play. Boots darted into the library ahead of Annie, staking her claim to the cozy reading chair by kneading the cushion with her front paws, and then settling down to watch the work. Annie surveyed the progress she and Alice had made, relieved the step stool would not be needed for the rest of the task. Only the lowest three shelves remained to be sorted, a substantial portion of them stuffed with Charles Holden's veterinary journals. Many of the navy blue covers were frayed along the edges from years of wear. Annie turned to the remaining reading material, saving the journals for last.

The majority of the books that would catch a child's eye already sat on the lower shelves, but they had been scattered from one side of the room to the other. Removing more books that bordered the area Alice had cleared, Annie made room for the new arrivals. The stacks beside the reading chair, now occupied by Boots, were growing as high as the armrests. The cat raised her head and pierced Annie with a disgruntled look as another six inches were added to the book wall.

Annie chucked Boots under the chin. "Boots, are you worried I'm going to turn you into a feline Rapunzel, hidden away in a tower of books? I promise to rescue you before the situation gets that bad." Boots, apparently not taken with the idea of being rescued, sprung lightly off the chair to reposition herself on top of the large cluttered desk. She stretched her hind legs, one after the other, before curling up again, setting off a domino effect among the clutter on the surface. A mug from the University of Maine, where Annie's grandfather had sometimes lectured, stuffed with pens, pencils, and a letter opener was the first to topple. Before Annie could clamber over the stacks of books, the letter opener had pushed against and collapsed a frame encasing a crayon drawing of Grandpa in his white lab coat, holding a hedgehog. In its turn the frame shoved against a box carved from dark wood, pushing it to the tipping point over the edge of the desk. Annie's hand stretched out to catch it, a couple seconds too late. It tumbled to the floor, the impact throwing off its lid.

"Boots!" Annie scolded as she bent to retrieve the box and lid, and gather the spilt contents. "What is it with us and boxes?" Grandpa had brought the box home from his travels during World War II. It was intricately carved from mahogany and was accented with genuine ivory, the inside padded with rich red velvet. Annie had always wondered if the beauty of that box had been what sparked Grandpa's hobby of carving. She scooped up the bits of paper scattered on the floor, glancing at them one by one. Most were notes of appreciation from relieved animal owners, a few receipts from local stores, and a few index cards filled with Gram's handwriting. Annie flipped through the cards, delighted to see they were some of her grandmother's most beloved recipes. The last one excited Annie the most. "Boots, you're forgiven. I found Gram's rose-hip jelly recipe!"

Boots trotted through the library door and down the hall, having had enough of the booby-trapped library. Annie followed her into the kitchen to restore the recipes to their original place on the baker's rack, the jelly recipe lying on top. If the rose hips had not needed a couple more days before reaching their peak, she would have abandoned the library to make jelly. But Gram had taught her well; rushing never made the best jelly. So she brewed a new cup of tea and carried on with her chore. After returning the desktop to its pre-Boots condition, Annie finished adding the rest of the books for the children to the area she had cleared. One of those books was *The Jungle Book*. Annie positioned it at the end of a shelf where it would be easy to find on the day she felt John and Joanna were ready to enjoy the stories.

Satisfied with the new children's section, Annie dug into shelving the books stacked around the reading chair. The variety of titles she read on the spines reminded her of how far flung her grandparents' interests had been. No wonder there had never been a moment of boredom during her summers at Stony Point. Once the reading chair had been liberated from the surrounding wall of books, Annie decided to give her back and knees a little break. She allowed herself some time to leaf through some of her grandfather's journals. In spite of the aura of cozy clutter in the library, his journals were meticulous, organized chronologically. Annie thought back to her conversation with Cecil and calculated in which years the journals were most likely to mention her new acquaintance. Pulling those journals off the shelf and stacking them on the side table, Annie settled into the reading chair.

For the next hour Annie was engrossed in her grandfather's adventures as a small-town veterinarian. With an economy of words, the journals told of filling out rabies certificates for disgruntled dog owners in December before they expired on New Year's Eve, detecting stomach ulcers in an alpaca, setting a leg of a Persian-mix cat that had not quite made it to the other side of the road. Then, Annie's eyes rested on the first mention of Cecil. "Cecil Lewey came along to assist on call to Hanover Farm. Ram. Calm and strong. Cecil, that is. Did not flinch when Percy tried to butt down the posts. Will offer him more work." Annie did not understand enough of the technical terms her grandfather had used well enough to know what had been ailing Percy.

Annie read enough to increase her appreciation for Grandpa's knowledge, skill, and his giving heart. She also was reassured she had been wise to pursue a different career path. Her teacup was long empty. Careful to keep the journals in the correct order, Annie began to put them back in their place. While the journals had been off the shelf, the books around them had shifted. Annie pushed the books to the left to make room again, holding them back with her left hand. She was reaching for the journals when she noticed a slip of white winking between the dark wood shelf and a book. Raising the book, Annie gently pulled the paper free. Her breath caught as she realized it was the same kind of delicate writing paper she had found in the birch-bark box. And it was torn.

Annie turned it over. The first line was the last line of the second verse she had read so many times:

How would you thrive?

Sister Rabbit, thicket thriving

Rain nurtures the chokeberries you eat.

If love took you to ocean deep,

How would you thrive?

There was a third stanza:

Sister White Deer, forest leaping

Come, bring your power to aid me now.

For love took me from all I know.

I cannot leap.

And there, below the third verse was a name, Clara Stewart, followed by the year the poem was written—1904—and two words, "mikwid hamid." Those words seemed strangely familiar to Annie, but she couldn't remember why. Had she seen it at the museum? No, it was during her visit with Cecil! Those were the Passamaquoddy words Tomah Joseph sometimes etched into his carvings. Annie strained to recollect the translation. *Remember me*, she thought. *Wasn't that it?*

The name, however, did not sound familiar. Running through the different Stony Point families she had met over the many months, Annie could make no connection.

A glance at the clock told her how quickly the time had fled while she worked; Alice was likely to be home from her sales meeting. Annie grabbed the telephone and called her neighbor.

"Hello?" Annie felt a surge of relief when Alice's cheerful voice spoke in her ear.

"I'm so glad you're home!" Annie blurted.

"So am I." Alice chuckled. "But I suspect we have different reasons. What's yours?"

"I made two discoveries while organizing in the library today. I found the rest of the poem—with a signature and date, no less."

"Seriously? In that library, you've accomplished the equivalent of finding the needle in a haystack! Who signed it?"

"I don't recognize the name. The date on the poem is 1904. It's in the same handwriting and the ink looks identical, so I don't think a different person added it at a later time. Have you heard of a Clara Stewart?"

"Clara Stewart. Stewart." Alice paused to think. "There's a Starrett family out at the end of Elm who have been here for ages, but that's as close to Stewart as I can come up with. We need to ask Stella, Gwen, and Ian. Their families have been in Stony Point much longer than most."

"The club meeting tomorrow will be an exciting one, for sure," said Annie. "Maybe by the end of it we will know who the collar first belonged to and will be a step closer to finding out how it ended up in the attic of Grey Gables!"

"Make sure you bring the last part of the poem with you tomorrow," Alice said. "You mentioned two discoveries. What was the other one?"

"Thanks to Boots, I found Gram's rose-hip jelly recipe! She knocked the mahogany box off the desk, and there it was."

"Sounds like Boots has earned her treats for the week, instead of a scolding. And just in time for the first crop of hips. If I help you pick them, will that earn me a couple jars of jelly?"

"You realize you will be running the risk of getting a mediocre reward for your work, don't you? I've never made jelly without Gram being right there with me," Annie reminded her friend.

"I'm banking on the probability that the jelly-making gene has skipped a generation," declared Alice. "And besides, with Betsy's recipe, how can it go wrong?"

"Well, it is true Mom wasn't one to bother with making jelly. I guess we'll know soon enough," Annie reasoned. "The hips should be ready any day, possibly even tomorrow. They were close when I checked them last."

"Give me a heads-up when you know it's picking day. I'll use my comp time from working so hard on Saturday and give myself some time off. It's one of the perks of being self-employed."

"I had to butter up my boss for time," Annie said with a smile. "It wasn't too difficult; I had a pretty good relationship with the boss. I'll let you go recuperate from your meeting. I want to get more done on my pillow tonight. Maybe it will help me figure out what other options I might have, if Kezi thinks there is a problem with my design."

"I just hope there are no big issues with mine. I have no idea what to do if I have to start with something new! OK, time to go distract myself until bedtime, or I won't get to bed early enough and will be late for the meeting."

"We can't have that!" Annie feigned horror. "A hot cup of chamomile might help too. See you tomorrow."

"I already put the water on. But just in case, you might want to call me around nine.

14

Annie hummed as she rounded the corner onto Main Street, the mid-morning sun glinting off the windows of A Stitch in Time and The Cup & Saucer. The glass doors of the movie theater were recessed too far back for the rays to reach, but the brick entry looked burnished. She squeezed the Malibu into a space in front of the hardware store. Getting out, she waved to Mike Malone, out performing his daily ritual of sweeping the sidewalk.

"Good morning, Annie," he called. "How are those storage containers working for you?" He drew his broom toward the small pile of debris one last time, and then turned to grab a long-handled dustpan.

"They're working great, Mike," Annie answered. "But they filled up too fast! I'm going to need a passel of them before I get Grey Gables anywhere near organized."

Mike swept the pile into the dustpan with economic strokes. "I can round up plenty more for you." He glanced at his watch. "You might want to hurry, or Stella will start without you."

"She just might at that. Thanks, Mike!" Annie grabbed her tote, glanced both ways along Main Street and jogged across to the shop. Jason smiled and tipped his hat in answer to her quick wave as she hurried past where he leaned against the Lincoln. Breezing through the door of the shop, she was surprised to see she was not the last one to arrive. Gwen's usual chair sat empty.

Alice patted the seat beside her. "How come you're late? You called me right at nine like I asked."

"Let's just say that sometimes having a cat isn't any different from having a toddler and leave it at that," said Annie. "Isn't Gwen coming?"

Everyone looked to Stella. "Gwen had certainly committed to being here," Stella answered. "She has the portfolio with the designs and comments from the curator. This is quite uncharacteristic."

"It sure is," said Peggy. "I hope Lisa didn't give Gwen her cold. Lisa was pretty miserable for several days."

Alice shook her head. "I'd think Gwen would be the last one to catch it. The rest of us—except maybe Stella—are at the diner much more often than Gwen is."

"Gwen might forgo a meeting due to illness or some other household snafu, but she would definitely inform someone first. She hasn't called here on any of our cell phones," said Mary Beth.

"I hope there's no emergency," said Annie. "Should we give her a quick call?"

Alice took her cell phone out of her purse. "I will." The members kept quiet as she dialed and waited for an answer. When there wasn't one, she left a message. "Gwen, it's Alice. We're all here at the meeting, hoping you're just running a little late. If there's anything we can do to help, please let us know. Bye."

"We should start the meeting, so Peggy can get back to work," said Mary Beth once Alice had ended the call.

"Stella, can you share with us everything you remember?" All the club members knew Stella's mind was likely to be more detailed than the notes in the portfolio that was still in Gwen's possession, wherever she was.

"Of course," said Stella. "Our time with the curator was very profitable. Kezi asked me to send her best wishes to all the members for undertaking this project. The designs pleased her very much."

"Oh, I'm so relieved!" Peggy wiped imaginary sweat off her forehead with a flourish. "Does this mean leaving out the geometric thing was OK?"

"Kezi gave us an overview of the use of the double-geometric shape in American Indian tribes of Maine and the northeastern United States. Quite interesting. Peggy, the shape has not been linked to any precise symbolism that makes its use necessary, especially in combination with the stars and cattails you want to use." Stella paused as Peggy danced in her seat with joy. "Kezi also appreciated your color choices. Red and yellow are prominent in the color palette of Abenaki art."

"Mary Beth, look for me during my break tomorrow," said Peggy. "I'll be picking out my red and yellow fabrics. Thank you, Kezi!" She blew a kiss toward Bar Harbor.

"You know, I think your trip yesterday was well worth it, Stella, if only to see Peggy so excited about her quilt!" said Kate, who had been quiet until that moment. She had placed herself as close to the front room as possible to listen for the shop phone, should it ring, or any customer who might arrive. She knew Mary Beth needed to hear the feedback about the projects.

"I agree with Kate," Mary Beth said. "You and Gwen have done us all a great favor."

Stella inclined her head, a small movement to acknowledge the gratitude. "Kate, I'll give the comments about your design next, so you can be free to help customers whenever it's needed."

"Thank you, Stella," answered Kate.

"The curator thought your pattern speaks eloquently to the importance of indigenous trees in the lives of the American Indian people of Maine."

Kate let out a deep breath. She hadn't realized she'd been holding it. "Peggy, I'm as relieved as you are."

"Kezi only cautioned—if you decide to add any beading—that you make sure you don't give the pattern a Christmas-tree look."

"Personally, I think the pattern is stunning enough without any embellishment," said Alice. "And you know I love your beadwork.

"My thought has been to not use any beading or ribbon or anything else," Kate said. "These comments have cemented that plan." The bell over the door of the shop chimed. Like spectators at a tennis match all the heads in the club circle turned toward it, wondering if Gwen had at last arrived. But instead, a woman and a teenage girl who shared the same color of light brown hair entered the shop. Everyone smiled to hear the first reaction.

"What a cozy, homey place!" The mother exclaimed, as she looked around at the displays Kate and Mary Beth spent hours each week updating and refreshing. "And the colors! Gorgeous!"

"It's almost as bright as my room, Mom." The daughter nudged her mother's arm, and pointed at the crochet section. "They have tons of crochet stuff."

"That's my cue," whispered Kate. She hurried to the front to speak to the newcomers. "Hello! Welcome to A Stitch In Time."

"We were so happy to see your shop," said the mother. "We're on a cross-country trip, and my daughter has been working on a crochet project she started at camp. I know nothing about crochet, I'm afraid."

The daughter carried on from there. "I'm done, but I don't know how to finish it. Can you show me what to do next?" She lifted a canvas bag up to show Kate.

"And maybe we can pick up another project for the trip home too," added the mother. Alice and Annie smiled at each other when they noticed the woman's hand reach out to feel the skeins of yarn sitting on a display near her. They could never resist the beckoning of the fiber either.

Stella turned her eyes back within the circle, signaling for the continuance of the meeting. "Shall we resume? Alice, your pattern looks great, according to Kezi. She simply said to keep in mind while you're creating the pattern on cloth that symmetry is important. Be meticulous in your stitch counting."

"If that's all the curator had to say, I'm thrilled!" Alice responded. "I'm no Betsy, but counting I can do."

Before anything else could be said, the door set off the chime again. It wasn't customers this time; instead Jason entered with something tucked under his right arm. He strode toward Stella, immune to the look of irritation she shot in his direction. "Now Jason," she started her scolding.

"Hold your fire," Jason said. "Mr. Palmer just asked me to deliver this to you. He said you'd need it for the meeting." He held out Gwen's leather portfolio to her.

"Did John say anything about Gwen? Is she ill?" asked Annie.

"He didn't say much," answered Jason, "only that I needed to bring the portfolio to the meeting right away."

"I'm glad to have my design back," said Alice. "But I'd also like to know if Gwen is all right."

"I think I'll pop in on John at the bank after the meeting and ask him about Gwen," said Annie. "One mystery at a time for the group is quite enough."

"We will conclude in good time and allow everyone to get along to their commitments," Stella insisted. Jason took that as his dismissal, and he nodded his farewell to the ladies and left to return to his post near the Lincoln. Stella continued, "Annie, Kezi was pleased with your design and how your color choices reflected the more contemporary urchin baskets in the museum. She agrees the round pillows would highlight the urchin pattern better than a flat piece. She also thanks you for your willingness to send your artifacts for her to examine. The impressions she shared with you last week were confirmed with the closer look." Stella bent down to reach underneath her chair, retrieving Annie's zippered tote bag.

Annie took the tote bag from Stella's hand. "This is so exciting! Now we know the dates of the box and collar could coincide with the date on the bottom of the poem. Now we have to figure out if they were family heirlooms for Clara, or if she found them somewhere."

Peggy blurted, "Who's Clara? What date?"

"That's what you get for being late, Annie," said Alice. "You didn't have a chance to share your news."

"Peggy, I don't want to make you late to work, so here's the short version," said Annie. "While I was cleaning in the library yesterday, I found the bottom part of the poem. Besides having the last line of the second stanza, there was a third stanza, and it was signed and dated! 'Clara Stewart, 1904.' There was also a Passamaquoddy phrase below the signature that means 'Remember me.'"

"Clara Stewart, eh?" Peggy glanced at the clock on the wall across the room and stood, obvious reluctance on her face. "1904. Drat, I have to get back or Jeff will give me grief. But I'll ask around about Clara. Some of the lobstermen's families have been around way before 1900, and they know the other families up and down the coast."

"Peggy Carson, P.I. is on the case!" Alice cheered. "But before you dash out, Peggy, we should check with Stella first. Stella, do you recognize the name?"

"I know some Stewarts in New York," answered Stella, "but I don't know of any here in Stony Point. It would be a long shot; however, I'll check with my friends."

"OK, Peggy, you have free rein to ask about," said Annie. "I'm thankful for all the help I can get!"

"You betcha! Bye, everyone." Peggy bustled out the door before Stella could call her back to give her the design for her quilt from the portfolio.

"Has there ever been a hurricane named Peggy?" Annie asked. Even Stella could not keep the hint of a smile from her face.

"I don't know, but if there has been, it couldn't outdo our Peggy," said Mary Beth. "Stella, I'll take Peggy's design. I'll drop it off to her before I head home." Stella opened the portfolio, located Peggy's, and handed it to Mary Beth.

When Stella had given out all of the designs, Annie offered to return the portfolio to John, as she still planned to pay him a quick visit to ask about Gwen. Alice realized the discussion of one pattern had been missed. "Stella, we haven't heard anything about your piece. What are you using for your inspiration?"

The older woman answered with a tone as close to nonchalant as she ever attained. "I chose water as my inspiration, for obvious reasons, and I'm knitting a scarf."

"After seeing that flame pattern you stitched, I can imagine how lovely a water scarf will be," said Mary Beth. "The yarn you chose is perfect. We'll adjourn our meeting now so we can all get to work!"

Alice reached into her purse for her keys. "With Kezi's help—and Stella and Gwen's too, of course—we can all work on our projects at next week's meeting. Watching them grow will be exciting. And Annie, try not to be late." The friends shared a laugh as they walked to the front of the store, where Kate was ringing up the purchases for the mother and daughter. Outside, Alice and Annie went in opposite directions, Annie toward the Stony Point Savings Bank and Alice to her car, which she had parked on Maple Street. Annie walked past The Cup & Saucer and had just crossed Oak Lane when she saw Gwen emerge from the bank.

"Gwen! We missed you at the meeting! I … " Annie's voice trailed off in surprise as her friend put her head down and hurried to her car without answering. Gwen yanked open the car door, ducked inside, and pulled away from the curb as though Annie was a mugger, not a friend. Annie paused in front of the library, trying to make sense of what had just happened. The only thought she had was that some family emergency had occurred and decided to follow her original plan to see John. *It must be something critical to have had such an effect on Gwen*, she thought.

Arriving at the bank during the late morning lull before customers came to do business on their lunch breaks, Annie was hopeful John would be available for a quick conversation. She approached the long prominent desk she knew to be John's and looked around for him. The large main room was quiet.

A meeting room door across the lobby opened. Annie was relieved to see John, president of the bank, emerging and started to wave. Her hand dropped when he looked straight at her—almost through her—narrowed his eyes, and marched over to a teller's booth. Leaning over the counter he spoke quickly to the teller. The employee nodded and placed a "window closed" plaque on the counter. As John marched back to the meeting room, the woman hurried over to Annie.

"Hello there, Mrs. Dawson. May I help you?" she asked competently.

"Uh, well, Melissa, I came to speak with Mr. Palmer on a private matter," Annie stammered.

"I'm sorry, Mr. Palmer is very busy. He won't be available all day."

"Oh." For a moment Annie was too startled by the obvious

snub to put together a proper response. "Thank you. Have a good afternoon." She turned to leave, working hard to keep a smile plastered on her face until she made it through the lobby area and out the front door.

15

Outside the bank, Annie leaned against the corner of the building, trying to draw strength from its bulk to deal with the shifting emotional winds of her morning. Closing her eyes, she hoped the breeze would cool the excessive warmth of her cheeks.

"That's one way to be a pillar of the community," the cheerful voice of Ian Butler spoke into her ear.

"You could call me Ms. Buttress, except it's not true," Annie said, keeping her eyes closed.

"What's not true?" Annie felt Ian's hand touch her shoulder.

Opening her eyes, Annie glanced at Ian's concerned face before lowering her gaze. "I seem to have a knack for throwing things off balance, rather than being a support. Why do I keep doing that?"

"Before we explore that question, could I interest you in a cup of coffee?" asked Ian. "I just finished a meeting at the Community Center about the Harvest on the Harbor celebration, and I could use a cup. You can tell me what happened along the way, if you'd like. I was given these hearty ears for a purpose."

Annie saw the wisdom of sharing the upsetting details before entering The Cup & Saucer. She moved away from the building where John, always a pleasant though slightly formal friend to her, in a moment had put up walls thicker than any New England fortress. Glancing back at the door of the bank and then around her to assure herself they were alone on the sidewalk, Annie described her experience with the Palmers to Ian.

"Sounds like your morning took a deeper plunge than the Excalibur," said Ian, referring to the highest roller coaster in Maine and all of northern New England. "I've known John and Gwen all my life. Gwen has never behaved in that way, as far as I know."

"Obviously, I haven't known her very long, but I thought we had become good friends. She's always enthusiastic whether encouraging me with my crochet or helping with my mysteries." Annie paused to aim a distracted smile at a Stony Point couple walking past them, fingers entwined, laughing at some private joke. She lowered her voice to continue. "Gwen lives and breathes for community. What could I have done that she would run from me?"

"Annie, if you hadn't told me about your visit to the bank, I'd be certain you weren't involved in any way with Gwen's emotional state," Ian said. "As it is, I'm completely perplexed. But, no matter how tempting it might be, trying to force the Palmers to communicate with you right now would be futile, in my opinion." Ian took one last step and then stood still. They had arrived at the diner.

"Ian, I know you're right. I learned that the hard way during LeeAnn's teenage years. Doesn't make it any easier, mind you," Annie said ruefully, lifting a hand to tidy her hair before going inside. "After thinking through all the contact I've had with Gwen or John over the last couple of weeks, I know I haven't done anything to offend them. At least my heart can rest on that fact."

"Good. Then my suggestion would be to come up with a nice distraction." Ian reached out an arm to open the door. "I even have an idea for one." Pulling open the door, he smiled into Annie's green eyes, pleased to see some of the worry clouds drift out of them.

"Does it involve recruiting me for the Harvest on the Harbor committee?" Annie guessed. "Need another pumpkin carver?"

"Hey, I like that idea, the first one. I'm not completely comfortable with the idea of you and large carving knives. I heard about what you did to those window screens last spring." Ian gestured toward an empty booth. Peggy hurried over to them as soon as they were settled.

"Hi, Annie. Mr. Mayor. What can I get for you?"

"Tea for me, Peggy." Peggy waited, but Annie added nothing more to her order.

"Is that all?" Peggy peered down at her friend. "Annie, you're going to shrivel up lighter than one of those tumble-weeds from your home state, and we'll have to hang lobster traps over your shoulders to keep you from being blown into the sea!"

"Now there's a New England fashion statement for me!" Annie said. She gave Peggy what she hoped was a reassuring smile. "Don't worry. As soon as I'm hungry I promise to eat enough to keep me grounded." Never mind that she expected that her appetite would be slow to arrive after this morning.

"You'd better," Peggy grumbled, and then shifted her eyes to Ian. "Mr. Mayor, you'd best not disappoint me."

"How about coffee and a tuna salad on rye?" answered Ian.

"With lettuce and tomato. It'll do." Peggy gave a short nod. "Cook just pulled a huge apple-cranberry crumble from the oven. Should I get you some for dessert?" Peggy's look dared the mayor to decline her offer.

"I have a long afternoon of work, and it would be a shame to tackle it without apple-cranberry crumble."

"Wise man, our mayor. Be right back with your drinks." Peggy left the table to hurry to a booth where a man in a chambray work shirt was waving his coffee cup at her.

As soon as she turned around, Annie leaned forward and wagged a finger at Ian. "I'll have you know window screening is a very temperamental material compared to pumpkins."

Ian caught Annie's hand as it moved in front of him and gently turned it over between his two hands. He brushed a thumb over the faint white line that ran vertically from the middle of Annie's wrist to the bottom of the palm. "Where did this scar come from?" He kept his voice low.

Pretending to ignore the bright flush fanning over her features, Annie answered stubbornly, "Not a pumpkin." Ian continued to hold her hand between his, waiting for her to continue. "It wasn't a suicide attempt or anything, if that's what you're thinking." The soft brush of his thumb began to stir up tingles she'd just as soon not have in the middle of The Cup & Saucer. "OK! It was a watermelon. I was slicing a watermelon. And I was a teenager!" She glanced wildly over Ian's shoulder to see Peggy heading their way again. "Peggy's coming. Please give me my hand back," she whispered in a panic. Ian moved his hands upwards and for one terrifying moment she thought he was going to raise her hand to his lips. She would never hear the end of it from Peggy.

Then she realized her hand was free. And Peggy was placing her cup of tea where three hands had been a moment before. She attempted to speak normally. "So I won't be on pumpkin-carving duty," she blurted. "That leaves me more time for my crochet."

"Oh, Doc Witham and Chessey Cushman always do the carving, Annie. Wait until you see what they can do! Makes me feel a lot better about having surgery, if I ever need to." Peggy set Ian's coffee in front of him. "Your sandwich will be out soon."

"Thanks, Peggy." Ian smiled at her. Annie paid extra attention to the process of lemon squeezing and honey dripping so that she didn't come across as rude to Peggy. If she looked in her direction, it might encourage Peggy to continue the conversation. She might even have an observation on what had just happened, and Annie definitely did not want to go there. But Peggy surprised her by bustling off without further comment to take another order across the room.

"Annie, I'm sorry I teased you. I wasn't thinking about how it might look to Peggy."

"Teasing doesn't bother me, Ian," Annie responded. It was those pesky tingles she couldn't handle. She wondered how he had noticed the small, shiny scar on her wrist, but she certainly wasn't going to ask. "I'm still wobbly and not acting like myself."

"You're acting just fine." Ian took a gulp of his coffee. "Are you still interested in hearing what I actually do have in mind for your distraction? It involves no volunteerism of any kind."

"Sure." Annie clasped the teacup between her hands, willing the warmth of the ceramic to calm her.

"How about a day out on a Butler boat for some whale watching? It would get you out of town, as well as give you a chance to take photos to send to John and Joanna."

Ian's proposal set off two warring voices in Annie's head: The woman who thrilled at the idea of exploring more of the Maine waterways and sharing it with her grandchildren cheered, but the woman whose wrist still felt the gentle brushing shied away from the thought of a day in close floating quarters with no way of escape. Annie raised her cup and took a slow sip of tea, biding her time.

Ian continued. "Todd can take us out tomorrow afternoon, after the lobster run, and I was thinking of also inviting Cecil Lewey, if you don't mind." This new piece of information brought comfort to her second, more reticent voice and changed everything.

"Don't mind at all; taking Cecil is a wonderful idea," said Annie. "Tomorrow afternoon is fine with me. Do you want to call Cecil right now before your food comes?"

Ian pulled his cell phone from the clip on his belt and located Cecil's number on his contact list. Annie continued to focus on her tea, but she couldn't help feeling relief when Ian's next words indicated Cecil had answered the call. The call ended with Ian saying, "I'll pick you up at noon. Yes. I will." He hung his phone back on the clip as Peggy brought his plate of food.

Peggy stood still for a moment after setting the plate down, a sure sign a question was coming. "Annie, did you talk to Gwen? Is she OK?"

"No, Peggy. I wasn't able to get a hold of her, and John

was not available when I stopped in at the bank." Annie chose her words carefully.

"Huh. How strange. I'll have to ask Mary Beth, if she comes in later."

"Maybe she just had one of those days," said Ian before taking a bite of his sandwich.

Peggy cocked her head to the side. "You know, I never thought Gwen had 'one of those days' like the rest of us. Kinda silly of me."

"Not silly, Peggy," Annie assured her. "Not everyone is as obvious in their imperfections as, say, me."

"Ah, go on!" Peggy chuckled. "I'll get you some more hot water, Annie."

"It sounded like Cecil will be coming tomorrow," Annie said after Peggy had gone.

"Yes, he enjoys being on the water," responded Ian. "I can pick you up on my way to Ocean View, if you like."

"Can I meet you at the dock? I'll probably walk."

"Sure, we should be there by twelve fifteen. Do you know where Todd keeps his boat? We're using the lobster boat, so I hope you weren't expecting a yacht."

"I've seen Todd's boat at the dock. I'm sure I can find it. John would be more excited to see photos of a real lobster boat, or any kind of working boat, than a luxury one. I'm glad we're not going fancy."

"At least we don't have the same problem at the harbor as some waterfront towns. Some places with ledges too shallow for boats to dock used to need a bos'n's chair to bring people ashore."

"What's a bos'n's chair?" asked Annie.

"You've seen those big swings at carnivals that move in a circle, haven't you? The faster they go, the higher they swing out."

Annie smiled at the thought; she had loved riding them as a child. "Yes, I do. They always had them at the county fair."

"Picture one of those swings chained to a large boom. People would sit in the chair to be swung to and from the boat."

"Sounds like fun," said Annie, grinning as she pictured the process. "Though I'd be less than thrilled swinging around in the layers of long skirts and corsets women had to wear a hundred years ago."

"So you won't be working at any living-history museums any time soon?"

"No, sir! The closest thing to living history I'm going to do is use Gram's recipe to make rose-hip jelly." Annie glanced at her watch. "In fact, I should get going. I think the hips might be ripe enough today, and I don't want the day to get away from me. I might end up picking with a headlamp strapped to my Aggies cap." Annie stood.

Ian stood to escort her to the door. "Thank you for keeping me company while I ate. I'll see you tomorrow, Annie. I've got your tea."

"Thanks for the tea, Ian, and thank you for your help." Waving to Peggy, Annie left the diner and walked to her car. She lowered her car windows for the drive back to Grey Gables, craving the sea air against her face. Once home she paid a quick visit to the beach roses to check the ripeness of the hips. What looked like thousands of them were now bright red and firm, no longer hard, and Annie could see plenty were free of blemishes—perfect for her first batch of jelly. Returning to the house, she called Alice to let her know picking time had arrived. As she waited for her helper, she rummaged around for a couple of buckets and gardening gloves. Rose-hip harvesting was a thorny job.

Strolling to the rose bushes, Annie realized she had forgotten to tell Alice to bring gloves. She set the buckets down and turned toward the house to call Alice again, but she had only taken two steps when her friend appeared.

"Oh, good, you brought gloves," Annie said as Alice approached. "I was going to call you again."

"The autumn months are my busiest months for Princessa jewelry shows. I can't demonstrate my samples with my hands scratched from fingertips to wrist, can I?" Alice also wore her anorak, a smart choice to protect her arms from the bite of thorns and the chill of late afternoon. She slipped her Princessa-worthy hands into her gloves. "Let me at 'em."

Annie handed her a bucket and pointed to a large bush a few yards downhill. "Let's start with that one," she said, as she put her gloves on too. "It's so hippy we could call it voluptuous." They positioned themselves on opposite sides of the bush and began picking the bright red hips, leaving the orange ones behind to ripen more.

Alice placed a juicy hip in the bottom of her bucket. "Are you going to make the jelly tomorrow? I'm thinking of making scones for the big taste test."

"In the morning," Annie said, cupping a hand around a hip and pulling until, with a faint pop, it came off the stem. "I have to have it done by noon."

"Why?" asked Alice. "Are you going somewhere in the afternoon?"

"Yes, I am. I'm going whale watching with the Butler brothers and Cecil Lewey."

"That sounds fun. I'm a little surprised Ian is taking off during the week, though," Alice said, the bottom of her bucket covered with rose hips. "Uncharacteristic of him."

Annie reached deeper into the bush for a particularly delicious-looking hip, glad for her thick denim jacket. "Not as much as you might think. First, Ian said he and the commissioners just finalized the budget. He racked up tons of comp time, as you can imagine. Second, he was characteristically being kind to one of his townsfolk."

"Would that folk be Cecil or you?"

"Probably both, actually, but me in particular." Annie drew in a deep breath of sea air before continuing. "I had a bizarre experience after the club meeting, and Ian happened to see me while I was still upset." She told Alice the story of Gwen and John in full detail as rose hips plopped into their buckets at a steady rate. They moved to another bush when red hips grew scarce on the first bush.

Alice listened intently, not interjecting comments or questions as she often did. When Annie had brought the story to an end, Alice continued to pick the seed pods in silence for a few minutes. Then she paused in her reaching and plucking to look Annie in the eyes.

"Now I'm really puzzled," she said. "Last night, after I left your house, one of my hostesses called and begged me to meet her at the diner to bring her more catalogs. She insisted it couldn't wait until today. If it means more sales, I'll sacrifice, you know. When I was walking back to my car from the diner, I saw Gwen. We chatted for a few minutes, mostly about how helpful the people at Abbe Museum have been. But she wouldn't let me weasel out of her what Kezi had said about my design before the meeting. I teased her a little, saying that even though she was making me wait, I was not going to make her wait to hear your news. Then I told her about Clara Stewart and the year on the bottom of the poem. Her only reaction was, 'Oh.' That's it. I noticed Gwen's face go pale, and then she mumbled something about needing to go. Off she went like the town was burning down again." Alice shook her head and resumed picking.

"It certainly goes against the usual way information flows through our community," said Annie. "You told Gwen last night about Clara Stewart, and yet no one else mentioned it at the meeting before I said something. Peggy didn't even know!"

"Peggy had already left for the night, or I would have told her," Alice confessed. "Whatever the reason for all this strangeness, hurray for Ian for whisking you away for a change of scenery. Whale watching will fascinate you, unless you get seasick easily. Uh, you don't, do you?"

"I don't think so," answered Annie. "Wayne took me on a cruise for our twentieth anniversary, and I didn't have any trouble. But the Butler boat could fit in the cruise ship's swimming pools, so I really don't know how my stomach will react to being on a smaller boat on the Gulf of Maine."

"If you start to feel nauseous when the boat dips down waves and tilts back up them, make sure you keep your eyes on the horizon. It will help. Hey, how full do our buckets need to be?" Alice tilted her bucket far enough so Annie could see the amount of hips it held.

"I'm starting with a small batch, about six jars, so I need three cups of juice. Between the two of us, we have enough, I think. I won't know until I put the boiled hips through the jelly bag. If not, I'll have to come pick more in the morning." Daylight was quickly fading.

"Want some help? You have a lot of trimming to do," said Alice.

Annie was thankful for the twilight, the shifting colors hiding the small change of color to her face as she was reminded of her last conversation that involved knives.

"I'd love some help. I'll even feed you dinner while the hips simmer. Then the juice can strain overnight." The two friends took their buckets into the house to carry on Betsy Holden's sweet tradition.

16

First thing in the morning Annie checked the amount of juice the jelly bag had produced overnight. In autumn, before daylight savings time ended, Annie generally rose before the sun did. Alice shuddered at Annie's penchant for early rising, but Annie knew that, compared to the large community of fishermen in the area, she was a late sleeper. Even so, she still needed to flip on the kitchen lights when she made her way downstairs. One of Gram's sturdy pans sat on the kitchen counter with the metal tripod frame attached to the rim, holding the jelly bag firmly over it. At first glance it appeared the hips she and Alice had trimmed and boiled last night were sufficient for the juice needed, but the measuring cup would tell the full story.

Annie set her coffee to brew and pulled a quart-size measuring cup from a cabinet. Taking the jelly bag off the frame, she set both things in the sink. She poured the juice from the pan into the large cup, relieved to see it reach past the three-cup mark. As Annie admired the colorful juice, Boots padded into the kitchen, sat down about a foot from her and stared.

"Don't look at me like that, Bootsie. If Gram were here, she'd have done the same thing." Annie had closed the door to the kitchen to ensure the rose-hip mixture would not be sampled during the night. "I made sure you still had your water." She reached down to pet the top of the cat's head on her way to bring the water dish back from the hallway right outside the kitchen door. After rinsing the dish and filling it with fresh water, Annie replenished Boots's food dish, and the cat settled down to eat.

Annie set the oven to preheat at 200 degrees, and then prepared some oatmeal. Before sitting down to breakfast, she placed six eight-ounce canning jars on top of a baking sheet in the oven to sterilize and also put the lids in a Pyrex bowl and poured boiling water over them from the kettle. Then, after adding a sprinkling of wheat germ and flax, a dash of cinnamon, and a splash of milk over the oatmeal, Annie was ready to sit down to eat too.

Fortified by her "power oatmeal," as she liked to call it, Annie poured the rose-hip juice into a large wide pot on a back burner of the stove. She pulled several lemons from the refrigerator and squeezed until she had a half a cup of lemon juice. After adding it to the pot, Annie stirred in a package of pectin. While waiting for the mixture to come to a boil and the pectin to dissolve, she measured out three and a half cups of sugar. The high emotions of the previous day dissolved like the pectin granules in the warmth of the homey process. It all came back to Annie as though she had canned a batch with Gram last month rather than thirty years ago.

Once the mixture began to boil, Annie stirred in the sugar until it had also dissolved. The sweet tangy smell was beginning to perfume the large kitchen. The final ingredient to be added was a one-fourth teaspoon of butter, swirled in before Annie allowed the pot to come to a hard boil. The orangey pink mixture bubbled, circles rising in domes until they stretched themselves too thin and burst.

Once the hard boil began, Annie flipped the little minute timer that sat beside the stove and took the sterilized jars from the oven as the sand flowed from top to bottom. The last grain tumbled from the top and Annie took the pot off the burner to pour the jelly into the jars, leaving a quarter inch of headspace below each rim. After securing the lids and rings on each jar, giving the jars a water bath was the final step. As the jars cooled from their bath, Annie listened for the familiar popping sound that signaled the lids had sealed properly. Once they were lined up on the shelf of the baker's rack, Annie thought the jelly looked like jars of sunrise. So often she had seen the cheerful color splashed along the horizon as a day began.

Although the sun had risen while she was busy in the kitchen, Annie poured another cup of coffee and went out onto the porch to see what kind of mood the weather was in. Settled into a wicker rocker, Annie was pleased to see the sky was an easygoing blue with lazy white clouds that looked in no hurry to blow elsewhere. Fog could blanket the coast sometimes for days at a time, but as far as Annie could tell, this wasn't going to be one of those days. However, the weather could be as temperamental as Boots around here. One thing she knew for certain was that she would need to bring layers of clothes and wear plenty of sunscreen on her whale-watching adventure. Not only could weather change with breathtaking speed, but the gentle water of a harbor often bore little resemblance to what the locals called "a bit of chop" once a boat entered the Gulf of Maine.

A bit of chop. Annie sipped her coffee, thinking how well the phrase fit her experience of the last twenty-four hours. She could relate to how Peter and the other disciples had panicked on a stormy sea. Gazing to the right side of the porch over toward the harbor, Annie prayed for the grace to handle whatever was to come before "Peace, be still" reigned over the puzzling situation with Gwen and John. Sometimes "a bit of chop" can help clarify where our true comfort lies, Annie knew. Her coffee mug empty and her heart strengthened, Annie went back inside to work on her crochet project until the time came for her to leave for the docks.

****

Annie arrived at Todd Butler's lobster shack at the same time Ian and Cecil did. A few lobster boats were moored, having put in a full day's work on the water already. A grin spread across his face, Ian gave her a hearty greeting. As Annie was saying hello to him and Cecil, Ian stepped closer to her and took a deep breath. "Mmmmm, you smell wonderful, Annie!"

Annie laughed. "How can you tell? All I can smell is fish bait!"

"When you've been around the lobster shacks as much as I have, I guess you adapt to the smell. White smell instead of white noise, in a sense. But I have to know, what is that scent?" Ian started to lean even closer for another sniff but thought better of it.

"It would be a mix of rose-hip jelly and sunscreen, I think," said Annie, resisting the urge to giggle. She stole a glance at Cecil and saw that he was enjoying the exchange as though Ian was a precocious boy. "I made the first batch of the season this morning."

"If it tastes as good as it smells, may there be many more batches to come," Ian said, as the door to the lobster shack opened. Todd Butler strode toward them, pulling a battered cap over hair the same color as his brother's. It was longer with an unruliness Annie found hard to imagine on Ian.

"Hi, Annie, Cecil," Todd said. He nodded toward his boat, idling at the moor and ready for the trip. "We scrubbed her for you, and we're ready to go."

Todd was conscientious about keeping his boat properly maintained as a matter of pride, but Annie saw immediately why Ian had warned her not to expect luxury. Lobstermen worked standing up and seats often were considered a waste of space. Todd obviously was one of those who thought so.

"Choose your spot, Annie," Ian said, waving his arm to indicate the length of the boat. "Anywhere other than at the wheel, of course."

Annie eyed the different positions she could choose. In one corner stood a tall pair of rubber boots with a pair of hauling pants tucked into the tops, ready for the next morning of work. Annie looked for a position that would offer her a place to hold on once they left the harbor. She settled on the front of the boat close to the dashboard, where a strip of wood had been nailed to keep things from sliding off. Cecil placed himself just behind her left shoulder, while Ian stood next to Todd by the wheel. Todd coaxed the idling motor to a low roar and pulled away from the dock, with Butler's Lighthouse now in front of them.

Halfway through the harbor, Annie looked behind her

for a moment, taking in the vista of Stony Point as it spread up the hill from the water's edge. The contrast of dark evergreens, autumn colors of the early changing trees, and homes painted various colors from the light gray of Annie's home to blue and green and red, gave the seaside town a cheerful look of welcome.

"She'd make a perfect cover for a Thanksgiving Day card," said Ian with what Annie thought of as his "proud mayor" tone.

"Yes, if card companies still make those," Annie said, turning her gaze forward. "It seems like more and more each year Thanksgiving gets overrun by Halloween and Christmas." Two laughing gulls wheeled overhead, their distinctive cry communicating derision for that trend.

"The business owners of Stony Point have noticed it, too, Annie. They take pains to not jump the gun on the winter holidays. The Community Thanksgiving Dessert helps give them incentive to create Thanksgiving displays."

"And all those homemade desserts are something to be thankful for," Todd inserted, as he expertly navigated the boat through the narrowing passage from harbor to gulf, the lighthouse now looming over them from its cliff-top position.

"Cecil, do you and your family come to the Thanksgiving Dessert, or do they live too far away?" Annie asked. Her new friend had been standing with quiet ease, his body adapting effortlessly to the movement over the water.

"Yes, Annie, we do come. My son Martin and my daughter Nataline live with their families in nearby towns. That's how I ended up in Stony Point. I'm in between the two. If I had stayed on the reservation, I wouldn't see them much."

"Takes a fair pile of pies to feed the Lewey-Bingham crowd," said Ian. "The ladies love watching their creations being devoured with such zeal."

"Only the ladies bring the desserts?" Annie asked, mischief lurking in her eyes. "Don't tell me the mayor of our fine town freeloads on Thanksgiving."

"Ian goes nuts on Thanksgiving," said Cecil.

"He means that literally," Ian informed her. "I am the official roaster of chestnuts. The old-fashioned way, I might add."

"So you get to play with fire, eh?" said Annie. During the discussion, they had left the waters of the harbor, heading down east. Although the conditions were below "a bit of chop" rating, they were a good deal more turbulent than they had been in the harbor. The boat dipped abruptly while Annie was speaking, and her arms followed instinct, flinging out to find a hold. The "eh" rose in volume and pitch.

Ian moved toward her, but was waved off by an embarrassed Annie. "I'm OK, Ian. Just wasn't paying attention." She watched her three companions to see how they stood and moved with the motion of the boat. After a few minutes she got the hang of it and broadened her focus again.

"Cecil, I read some of Grandpa's vet journals this week," said Annie, switching gears. "You two had some interesting adventures. My favorite so far is the one about a bull named Milton."

Cecil laughed. "That animal was a good reminder of why I prefer the sea!"

"I want to hear your gadfly impression that was so effective. Will you humor me?"

Todd nudged Ian. “D’ya remember how the monster nearly pegged us?”

“I remember how I told you not to go in there, but you did anyway,” answered Ian. “What’s this about gadflies?”

“Just a trick I picked up along the way,” said Cecil. “Steers and cows hate gadflies, so I buzzed at Milton when Charlie and I’d had enough of him, like this.” Cecil emitted a buzz so authentic that it made Annie’s skin itch. “He hightailed it.”

“I wish we’d known that trick,” said Todd, shaking his head. “Would have saved my favorite hat.”

“And Mom a lot of gray hairs!” Ian said, laughing.

“Look starboard, Annie,” Cecil said. “A humpback feeding.”

Annie had learned that starboard was to the right of the boat, when facing the bow. A ring of aqua water, as bright as any she had seen in the Caribbean, bubbled. She gasped as the surface split, the giant knobby mouth of a whale rising up as it opened like a giant oyster. As it reached the crest, the mouth snapped shut and fell back into the water.

“There goes a hundred pounds of herring,” said Todd. “Bit of a snack, that.”

Annie leaned over the dashboard, keeping her eyes on the surface of the water. “I’ve read many times about the size of whales, but seeing one in front of me. Whew!” She reached in the pocket of her coat for her small digital camera. “Do you think it will come up again?”

“Takes more than a hundred pounds of fish to make a meal for a humpback,” said Cecil. “There’s a good chance he’ll be up again. Just look for the bubble ring.”

They didn’t have to wait long before the surface turned

that dazzling aqua again. Annie lifted the camera, snapping as many shots as she could. Before the next splashdown she remembered that her camera had capabilities for short videos and captured it. "John is going to be speechless. Well, no, he'll probably chatter about it to anyone who'll listen."

"Sometimes there are fin whales not too far from here. Are you OK with us moving along?" Todd asked after they had watched the feeding for a while.

Annie nodded, snapping a last couple of shots before the boat moved past the humpback. She kept her eyes roaming, scanning the surface of the water. A few minutes passed with no sign of more whales, so she relaxed her search, trusting that the three Maine natives would spot anything she shouldn't miss seeing.

"Cecil, I almost forgot to tell you," Annie said. "The Milton story wasn't the only thing I found while I was organizing Grey Gables's library this week. I found the last stanza of the poem I told you about, signed with the name of the author! Her name is Clara Stewart, and she dated the poem 1904."

"Ah, that's good." Cecil nodded, still standing ramrod straight with no signs of tiring. "If you contact the reservation in Point Pleasant, they can tell you if the name is registered with the tribe. If it is, there may be more information they can share with you. I was born in 1934. From the poem, I would assume that she had moved away from her people before she wrote it, well before my time."

"That's my assumption, as well," said Annie. "I'll go tomorrow." Then remembering how some agencies had been needing to cut their hours of operation, she added, "If they have regular operating hours tomorrow, that is."

"They will," Cecil assured her. "The tribal government follows the typical days of operation. They're closed for major holidays like Thanksgiving, Christmas, and New Year's Day.

"Do you visit the reservation often?" asked Annie. She was surprised how at home she now felt on the boat as it plowed through the light chop. They might have been having a visit in her living room at Grey Gables.

"I try to, when Martin or Nataline are going. Nataline's only daughter, Macey, lives there now, and we visit her as often as we can, for dance days or weekends." Cecil scanned the horizon line, a faint smile playing around his mouth. "Feisty one, she is. Went to business school for medical transcription. She always wanted to live at Sipayik as a kid. Nataline would challenge her about what kind of job she would find there. So she researched about jobs she could do from her home and found one. Her grandmother Rose was feisty too. Strong spirit. Weak heart, though."

Thankful for the sea spray that mingled with the tears forming in her eyes, Annie nodded her understanding. Wayne had been stronger than his heart too. "Did Gram and Grandpa know Rose?" she asked.

"They were both good friends to Rose and me. Many times when Rose was in the hospital, I'd come in to find Betsy sitting by her bed, cross-stitching and keeping Rose informed on whatever was happening."

"Cecil and Rose used to live in a cottage near where Wally and Peggy live," said Ian. "I used to detour past their place just to smell Rose's cooking. If I timed it right and made enough noise as I went past, sometimes I'd score a dinner invitation."

"I'm beginning to wonder if Stony Point elected a mayor who is part hound," said Annie, laughing.

"Fin whales at port," announced Todd. Annie saw a smooth line of whale back with a sleek dorsal fin rise out of the water and grabbed her camera just in time. The giant mammal exhaled, shooting a spout of moist air straight up like an exclamation point.

"Whoa!" she gasped. "They even breathe with power."

"I'm going to pull up as close as I can," said Todd. Look behind the whale's head for the chevrons when it surfaces again." He throttled up the boat with a light touch, inching closer. Annie leaned forward without thinking, instinctively trying to get as close to the fin whale as possible. The undulating movement of the whale captivated her. When the head broke the surface Annie squealed, "I see the stripes!" She kept staring. "It looks like there's a shadow over part of it, but nothing to make it. It's not from the boat."

"You're right. It's not a shadow," said Cecil. "Fin whales have asymmetrical coloring on their backs, light on one side and darker on the other."

"I could watch them all day long!" said Annie. "I never want to lose this astonishment at God's creation."

"If you want to be amazed, watch a humpback breaching," said Ian. "Fin whales aren't much for breaching."

"I've heard of a fin whale calf breaching in the Bay of Fundy," said Cecil. "But I've never personally seen it, and I've been on the water most of my life as a fisherman and guide."

They lingered to enjoy the fin whale for a long time. At one point it disappeared, and Annie wondered if it was time to explore another area. She had just turned to speak to Todd about it when the boat rocked from a jolt underneath. Annie grabbed at the dashboard, gripping the little wooden ledge Todd had made to right herself. "What's happening?" Visions of submerged ledges and reefs rushed into her thoughts, although she thought they were too far from shore for that.

"Look port!" Ian urged, as he steadied her with a hand on her shoulder. Annie caught the long shadow of the whale emerging from under the boat.

"Is it mad or just being neighborly?" she asked, catching her breath.

"It's being curious," answered Todd.

"Maybe now would be a good time to look for some breaching humpbacks," Annie suggested, only partially joking. The rocking boat reminded her the majestic giant wasn't tame, and such power so close to them, even if it was simply out of curiosity, sent a tendril of chill down her spine.

"Ayup," said Todd. He maneuvered away from the fin whale and gave some throttle. For the next hour they searched the water for signs of humpbacks or other whales, but saw neither flukes nor fins nor spouts. The sun was hovering low to the water when they all acknowledged that breaching was going to have to wait for another trip.

"I'm sorry, Annie," said Ian, as the boat sped toward Stony Point harbor.

"Sorry? Oh, Ian, you have nothing to feel sorry for," replied Annie. "What a gift y'all have given me today! I'm going to do what I can to make sure John can come whale watching next summer, including begging LeeAnn, if I have to."

"If you can get him to the Maritime Museum in November, I think John might do the job for you," Ian said, smiling with relief.

Annie patted the pocket in which her camera was nestled. "These photos will help too, I'm sure." The sea air was getting colder by the minute as the wind kicked up. Annie's coat had been enough to fight off the chill while the sun was higher, but now she fought the shivers, realizing one more layer of clothing might have been wise. She looked forward to gaining the harbor where the winds would be buffered.

They neared Butler's Point, the firs and pines black against the sunset sky of pinks, lavenders, and blues. Countless times Annie had stood on her porch to watch the play of sunrise colors over the water. It had been a long time since she'd seen it the other way around. It was no wonder to her why Gram and Grandpa had chosen to put down roots in Stony Point.

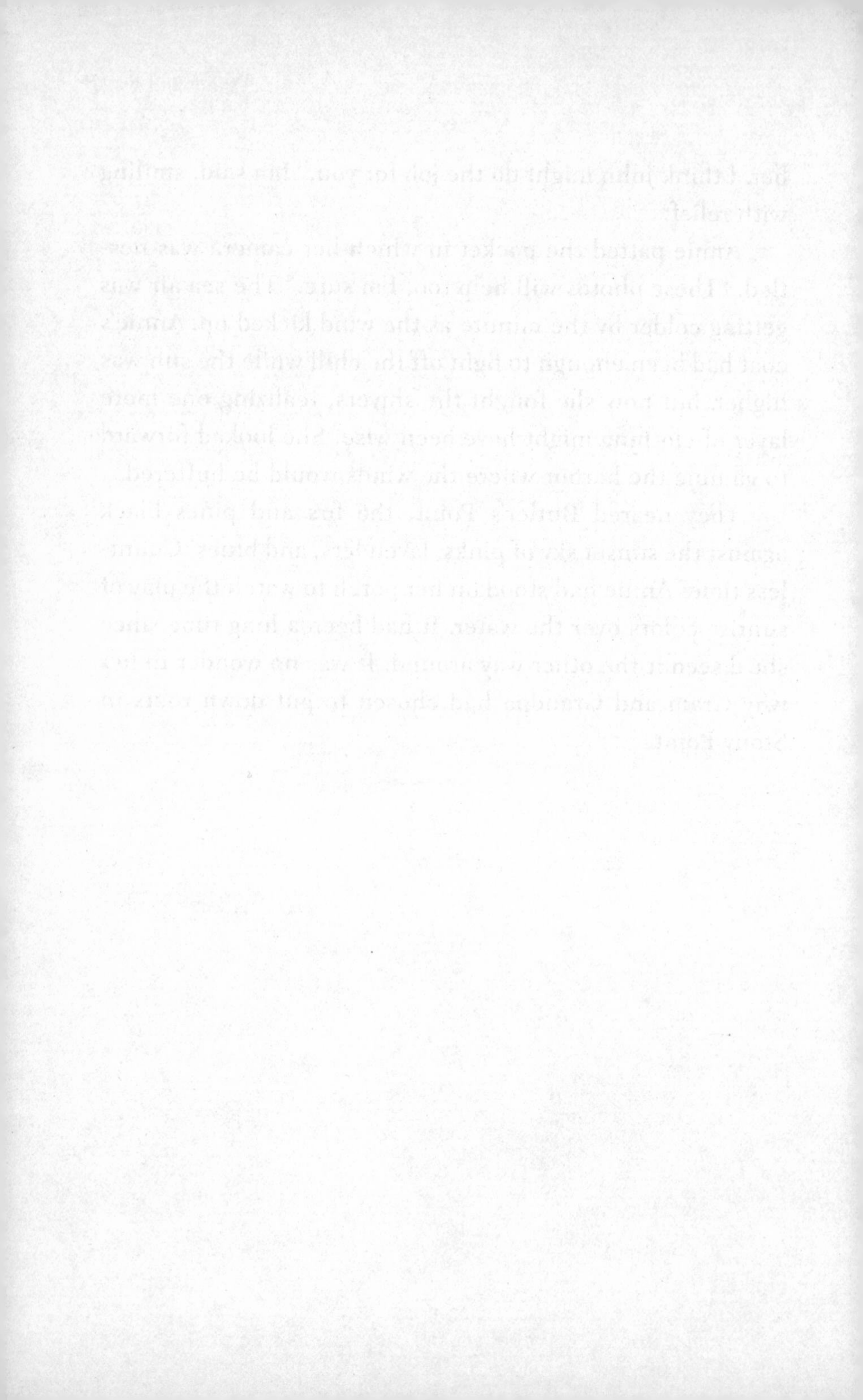

17

The morning after her whale-watching adventure—while the sun announced its imminent appearance by painting the canvas of sky with shades of cornflower blue, cerulean, melon, and yellow ochre—Annie placed the zippered tote containing the birch-bark box in the passenger seat of the Malibu and walked around to slide behind the steering wheel. She had several hours to drive and wanted to arrive at Sipayik before lunchtime. The meandering road of Route 1 beckoned her with its autumn splendor.

Remember, Annie, you're a woman on a mission, she told herself. *No stopping to explore until you finish at the reservation.*

She pulled out of the driveway, not surprised to see that the windows of the carriage house were still dark. Alice had been aghast during their phone conversation the previous night when she heard about Annie's early departure time. "The only thing that could get me out so early is fire raging through the house," Alice had declared. Annie was determined to find another method of luring Alice to experience a glorious Maine sunrise and toyed with ideas as she headed for Route 1 North.

Annie made good time winding through towns like Belfast, Bucksport, and Orland, stopping only once in Ellsworth to stretch her legs and grab some coffee at the 1950s retro Martha's Diner. The coffee was good, and she could tell by the crowd, the aroma, and snatches of conversations that it was a place worth revisiting when she had time to sit down for a meal.

Just after eleven o'clock Annie found the tribal government office at Sipayik on Route 190. A circular drive encompassed a grassy circle where two flagpoles stood, one flying the Passamaquoddy flag and the other the Stars and Stripes. Annie turned to the right and parked near the entrance of the long one-story building. Inside, the large central room was reminiscent of the offices of Annie and Wayne's dealership in Texas, with light painted walls, standard business desks outfitted with phones and computers, and a large copy machine against a wall with a large calendar from an Eastport Realtor hanging near it. Two women were standing beside one of the desks, their heads bent over an open file folder. They glanced up when Annie stepped over the threshold and one of them, whose ID badge identified as Janet, came to greet her.

"Hello. Are you from the university?" she asked pleasantly.

"Oh, no. I'm not." Annie stammered a little, caught off guard.

"Oops. We had a call from the linguistics department last week, asking if they could send another doctoral student for some research. Thought that might be you." From the good-humored squint of Janet's dark eyes under a glossy brown fringe of bangs, Annie got the feeling visits from academics were common occurrences.

"My university days are long past." Annie grinned. "But I *am* here to do some research, personal though." She told

Janet about her discovery in the attic and showed her the box and collar. "I'd like to find out if Clara Stewart is registered with the tribe. A Passamaquoddy friend suggested I start here."

Janet nodded to the other woman, indicating she could return to what she'd been doing before Annie came. "What's your friend's name?" she asked.

"Cecil Lewey."

A smile sprang instantly into Janet's eyes, fanning across her face. "*Cecil!* One of the best dancers I've ever seen. It would be a shame if I didn't help a friend of his."

Janet's eyes moved to the box and collar. "These are very personal heirlooms," she said. "What was the name again?"

"Clara Stewart," answered Annie. "I assume that is her married name. She was married in 1904 or earlier. I don't know her maiden name."

Janet moved to a desk with a computer and sat down at the keyboard. Her fingers flew over the keys, accessing the Passamaquoddy registry.

"Got something!" Janet exclaimed triumphantly. "1886, Clara Mitchell, born to William and Catherine Mitchell. She married Finlay Stewart in 1902. Let me see if any children are listed." Janet clicked the mouse a couple of times, and tapped in an additional search. "One child registered, Evelyn Stewart." Janet paused as she searched for later entries. "The line stops at Evelyn."

Annie jotted down the names and dates. "What was Evelyn's birth date?"

"June 23, 1906."

"Is there any way of knowing why a line ends?" Annie

asked. "Does the registry indicate if there are no more children or a premature death or anything?"

"Sometimes records are more detailed," Janet explained. "There is no year of death listed for Evelyn, though. That would suggest the family did not wish to keep registered with the tribe, or could not, for whatever reason. I can print out the family line before Clara, if you'd like."

"Oh, please do! That would be a great help," said Annie.

"Hmmm, looks like there's a Revolutionary War veteran in the family, a captain," Janet said as she prepared the information for printing. "Probably fought in the Battle of Machias." She swiveled her chair away from the desk and stood. Walking over to the printer, she pulled the printouts and handed them to Annie, who added them to her tote.

"I hope the information will help you find out more. I hope you can find the family members, if the line has continued."

"Thank you so much for your help, Janet." Annie reached out to shake her hand. "Having Evelyn's name and birth date gives me much more to go on and also strengthens my suspicions that the items are not from my ancestors."

Janet walked Annie to the door. "If you find more information on Evelyn's family line, please let me know. I'd like to update our records. And bring Cecil for one of the dance days. You'll both enjoy it."

"I'd love to come," said Annie. "Do you have a list of dates?"

"We always post them on our website." As Janet opened the door for Annie, in rushed a blast of cold air. They could hear the two flags out front snap in the wind. "Storm's kicking up."

"I'll do my best to stay ahead of it," said Annie, keeping

a tight hold on the tote. "Thanks again, Janet!" She hurried to the car, imagining the kind of storm that was coming. The dense fog the area was infamous for would be terrible to drive through. Annie decided to fill up her gas tank and pick up some lunch she could eat as she drove so she wouldn't have to stop again on the way home.

By four thirty Annie was pulling up the driveway of Grey Gables. She had driven through increasing cloud cover until she was about forty-five minutes outside of Stony Point, when the rain began. Pulling as close as she could to the door, Annie was still quite wet before she hurried under the shelter of the porch roof. "Why didn't you bring a slicker?" she chided herself. "Haven't you learned how tricky Maine weather is yet?"

Boots was stationed at the entrance to the living room when she opened the door. She padded over to Annie. "Hey, Boots! Did you miss me?" Annie said, bending down to give the cat a little loving attention. But Boots didn't love the dampness of her shoes and slacks, and scooted away back to the dry comfortable couch.

"Miss Persnickety!" Annie chuckled. "I'm going to change into comfortable dry clothes, make some dinner, and then will you be ready for a good cuddle? I'm sure not going anywhere on this wild night!" Boots closed one eye, tilted her head, and began licking a paw and then passing it over an ear. Annie had been dismissed to make herself presentable.

After making and enjoying a warm meal, Annie settled down with Boots on the couch, a cup of tea steaming on the side table next to her. She pulled out her crochet and set to work, hoping to finish and block the first pillow pieces. The rhythm of the alternating passes of Tunisian knit and purl work lured her into a state of relaxation after the tense ride home. Boots shifted her body until her back pressed lightly against Annie's leg. Annie paused long enough to run her hand along her sleek back, being careful not to allow any stray cat hairs to end up crocheted into the pillow.

The sound of the rain drumming against the house made her think of Janet's comment about Cecil and his dancing. Annie had been impressed with the ease Cecil had shown those hours on the boat, his body adjusting effortlessly to any movement of the vessel over the water, even the jolt from the fin whale passing under them. After so many years of making his living on the sea, Cecil understood its rhythms as well as he did the dances of his tribe. But Annie thought back to the first time she'd met Cecil and puzzled over something. His posture had been just as straight as it had been on the boat, but he had used a walking stick on their climb back up the stone steps. There had been no walking stick on the boat, and he had not leaned against the side of the boat or the dash or a friend. How could he do that for so many hours?

A ringing phone interrupted her mental gymnastics. Startled, Annie set her crochet back in the bag and lunged for the phone. "Hello?"

"Annie, it's Peggy." Peggy's voice was breathless, a rare state for someone used to bustling around at work while never losing a word in conversation.

"Hi, Peggy. Is everything OK?"

"No, it's not," Peggy answered bluntly. "The strangest thing just happened. John and Gwen were here at the diner for dinner." She paused. "They got into an argument, right there in the middle of their fish chowder. They were almost *yelling*, Annie!"

"That does sound very unusual for both of the Palmers," Annie said. *But,* she thought to herself, *it doesn't sound as odd as it might have last week.*

"Gwen was as white as her double-bleached tablecloths. I've never seen her like that. And Annie, I heard John use your name. More than once. Something about it all being your fault. Whatever he thinks you did, he's really mad about it. Do you know what he meant?"

Annie sighed. "No, I don't know what John was talking about, Peggy, but I think it must have something to do with the mystery about the box because Alice told Gwen about the new clue after she and Stella got back from the museum. Then, when I went to ask John if Gwen was all right after she missed the meeting, he refused to talk to me."

"Hmm. Well, you know we all like helping you with your mysteries. It gives us an excuse for snooping and adds a little excitement to the week. You have ended up with people mad at you before. I just never thought the Palmers would be."

"We're going to have to find other things to do for excitement, Peggy," said Annie, knowing already that snooping had never needed an excuse in Stony Point. "I'm through with mysteries, for good. I'm tired of being the spark that sets off all these emotional and relational fires. The town has burned down enough times in its history, it doesn't need me blowing hot embers everywhere."

"Aw, Annie, don't feel bad. It's not your fault—"

Annie jumped as someone banged on the door.

18

The insistent pounding at her front door jarred Annie into urgency.

"Peggy, I need to go. Someone's at my door. If you hear anything else about Gwen or from her, please let me know. Bye!" Annie placed the handset back in its charger and ran to the door. A blast of wind tried to wrestle the door from her grip. A man stood on the porch, his face shrouded in the shadows of a raincoat hood. Fighting the urge to slam the door, Annie spoke, voice raised to compete with the wind and rain. "Hello! How can I help you?"

A hand lifted and pushed back the hood. It was John Palmer. In spite of the strange occurrence in town Annie was relieved to see him.

"John! Please come in!" Annie widened the opening of the door, stepping back. John stamped his feet to shake off some of the water and mud, and stepped over the threshold, stopping just inside the door on the entry rug.

"You ask how you could help me," said John with a rusty hinge of a voice. "You can help by giving up your meddling ways!" His eyes darted around the foyer and hall until they rested on a portrait of Charles and Betsy Holden and narrowed. "Your grandparents were meddlers too!"

"Since everyone in Stony Point seems to know everyone else's business, I should fit right in, just like Grandpa and

Gram did!" Annie retorted. As frustrated as she was with John's accusation, Annie caught herself before her emotions got the best of her and tried a different angle. "John, Gwen has told me story after story of ways Gram was a blessing to others. She didn't seem to think that was meddling." Boots appeared near the top of the stairs, descending slowly one step at a time, as if sizing up the situation.

"Well, she does now!" John paused with his mouth open, gasping in air. Annie expected him to continue, but he didn't.

"Is Gwen in the car?" asked Annie. "Let's all sit down and talk about this."

"No!"

"Is that no to her being in the car or no to talking?" Annie tried to keep her voice as calm as possible, but calm was the last thing she felt, her heart pounding like a drum.

Uncertainty flickered in John's eyes, but he clamped his mouth shut.

"What I still don't know is what I've done to meddle in your business—or Gwen's." As Annie spoke, Boots stepped down into the foyer, padding forward to lightly brush against Annie's legs. Then the cat positioned herself between John and Annie with ears pricked sideways and her tail pointed at an angle toward the floor, ready to show aggression, if need be.

"Well, I'm not about to educate you!" John's voice heightened to a yell. He yanked the hood of his coat back over his head. "But don't you ever bring hurt or harm to my wife again." He jerked open the door, tossing back over his shoulder, "Better yet, go back to Texas!" The slam of the door reverberated from the door frame out along the wall.

Annie sank down to sit on the bottom step of the staircase, holding out a hand to Boots. The potential threat gone, Boots's tail lifted and her ears moved forward as she drew close to Annie for a rub. "Whew!" Annie exclaimed in an attempt to lighten the moment. "If John could swing a golf club like he swung that door, his golfing buddies would be impressed!" That didn't work, so she allowed the automatic movement of her hand over fur to calm her.

"I have to find Gwen, Boots. I don't think she was with John. If she's as upset as he is, she could be so vulnerable on a night like this." Annie gave Boots one last scratch under the chin before going into the living room for the phone. She punched in Gwen's cell phone number, wincing as she heard the rain splattering against the window like snowballs thrown by the wind. Gwen's voice mail greeting spoke into Annie's ear. Disappointed but not surprised, Annie left another message. "Gwen, it's Annie. Please call me. I'm worried about you."

As soon as she ended the first call, she dialed a different number. When her friend answered, Annie drew a sigh of relief. "Alice, thank God you're at home! I need your help."

"Then I'm glad I'm home too," said Alice. "What's up?"

"I just had the most awful visit from John Palmer, and it followed a phone call from Peggy with a strange story." Annie heard a beeping begin on the other side of the line. "Now I'm truly worried about Gwen."

"I can tell by your voice. Do you want me to come over?" Annie heard the beeping stop and the sound of Alice's oven door opening and shutting.

"Would you? It sounds like you're baking again."

"I was baking again. Just took the last of it out of the oven. Let me pull on my rain gear and I'll see you in a few."

As soon as Alice had shaken the rain from her clothing and shed her hat, coat, and boots, Annie led her to the living room and described her phone call from Peggy and John's eerie visit. When she was finished, Alice leaned an elbow against the arm of the couch, resting her cheek in hand. "How many years have I lived in Stony Point and have known John and Gwen?" she said. "Decades, and not once have I ever heard about or seen that kind of behavior from either one of them. They've always been the embodiment of self-control. At times I've hoped they would loosen up, let go some. But this is scary!" Boots sprang onto the couch between the two friends, kneaded the cushion under her front paws, and curled up for a nap. A hand from each side gently stroked the sleek back.

"What do we do next?" Annie asked. "My thinking is that Gwen was not with John when he came here; he looked insecure when I asked if Gwen was in the car. And if she felt like I had hurt her somehow—although I can't think of any way that I have—would she come anywhere near Grey Gables? I don't see it."

Alice gave a small shake of her head. "Neither do I. Did Peggy see how the argument ended?"

"I don't know. I had to end the call quickly when John knocked on the door. Banged, actually. Maybe we should call Peggy and see if she saw where they headed after they left the diner." Annie started to get up to retrieve the phone, but Alice motioned for her to stay put. She handed Annie her cell phone, pulled from the pocket of her jeans. "Speed dial number three."

Annie settled back against the couch cushion as the line rang. Peggy answered, "Ay, Alice."

"It's Annie, Peggy. Sorry to fool you. I won't keep you long. I was wondering if you could tell where Gwen and John were headed after the argument. Or did one of them say anything about where they were going next?" Annie wasn't sure how to word her questions differently, as she preferred not to mention John's visit.

"Let me think a minute, Annie." Peggy paused to run the scene through her mind. "Can't say I heard any place names, just John complaining about 'those Holdens.' Just as they were starting to get really loud, I think they realized folks were listening. They walked out quick like. I tried to peek out the window as long as I could. I saw John lurch over to the passenger door and open it for Gwen, still hotter than a hornet. But Gwen shook her head and backed away from the car. The last thing I saw was Gwen taking off down Main Street and John throwing up his hands. Then a big order came up, and I had to leave the window."

"Gwen must have been at wit's end to run off on a night like tonight."

"Don't ya know it! I see a lot at the diner, but I never expected to see John and Gwen going at it."

"Do you remember which way Gwen went on Main, Peggy?"

"Uh … yeah, south."

"Thanks for your help. I'll talk to you soon."

"No problem. I hope you can help Gwen work out whatever's bothering her. G'night, Annie."

"Good night, Peggy." Annie switched off the phone and handed it back to Alice.

"Well?" Alice said, slipping her phone back into her pocket.

"My hunch might be right. Peggy saw Gwen refuse to get into the car with John. She ran south on Main."

"That eliminates a few blocks of searching. It's something. Do you suppose Gwen just went home?"

"I don't know, but I think we should start looking there. If John went home from here, you're going to have to go to the door alone, while I hide in the car. My presence would not lend a calming atmosphere to your conversation with John." Annie stood up. "And we better not wait any longer."

Alice followed Annie into the hall. "How about we take the Mustang?" She didn't feel the need to explain why. Her boots stood at attention on the entry rug. She pulled them on first, before putting on her coat and hat.

"Sure," Annie answered quietly. "I think we can leave the top up tonight." Taking her long slicker off the coat rack standing against the wall, she buttoned it up to the top button. She stamped into the high rubber boots she had bought at Malone's once she decided to stay in Stony Point for a while. "My scoodie won't do for tonight's weather." Annie reached past the scarf and hood combination she had crocheted in a rich deep red with a light shimmer of gold and snagged a wide-brimmed rain hat.

"That scoodie rivals even Kate's creations for beauty, Annie," Alice said in an attempt to lighten the situation. Alice walked over to feel the soft, thick cashmere blend. "It's gorgeous and even practical for our windy Maine days. Rainy ones excepted."

Annie smiled her thanks and clapped the rain hat over

her hair. The two women went out onto the porch where curtains of rain cascaded from the edges of the roof.

"Ready? *Go!*" yelled Alice. They charged down the porch steps and across to the carriage-house driveway where the Mustang was parked. Alice pressed the keyless entry button on her key ring, and the pair dove into the car, slamming the doors as fast as they could.

"I hope Gwen's home!" Annie gasped. "This is no night to be out alone."

Alice agreed as she turned the ignition and slowly backed out of the driveway. The Palmers' home, Wedgwood, stood a short distance from Grey Gables. No cars stood on the driveway in front of the blue colonial, but the Palmers had renovated an old barn into a garage behind the house.

"I can't tell if anyone's home or not," said Annie. "You better go alone."

She watched anxiously as Alice ran up to the door of the meticulously maintained home and used the heavy brass knocker several times. After several minutes of waiting, Alice sprinted back to the car.

"If anyone is home, they are faking it very well," said Alice.

"I stared at the windows as you knocked," said Annie. "I didn't notice any movement or changes in lighting after you knocked. Let's just drive along some of the roads and make sure Gwen's not still out there. She may not want to see me, but mercy, how I hope we'll see her. And soon!"

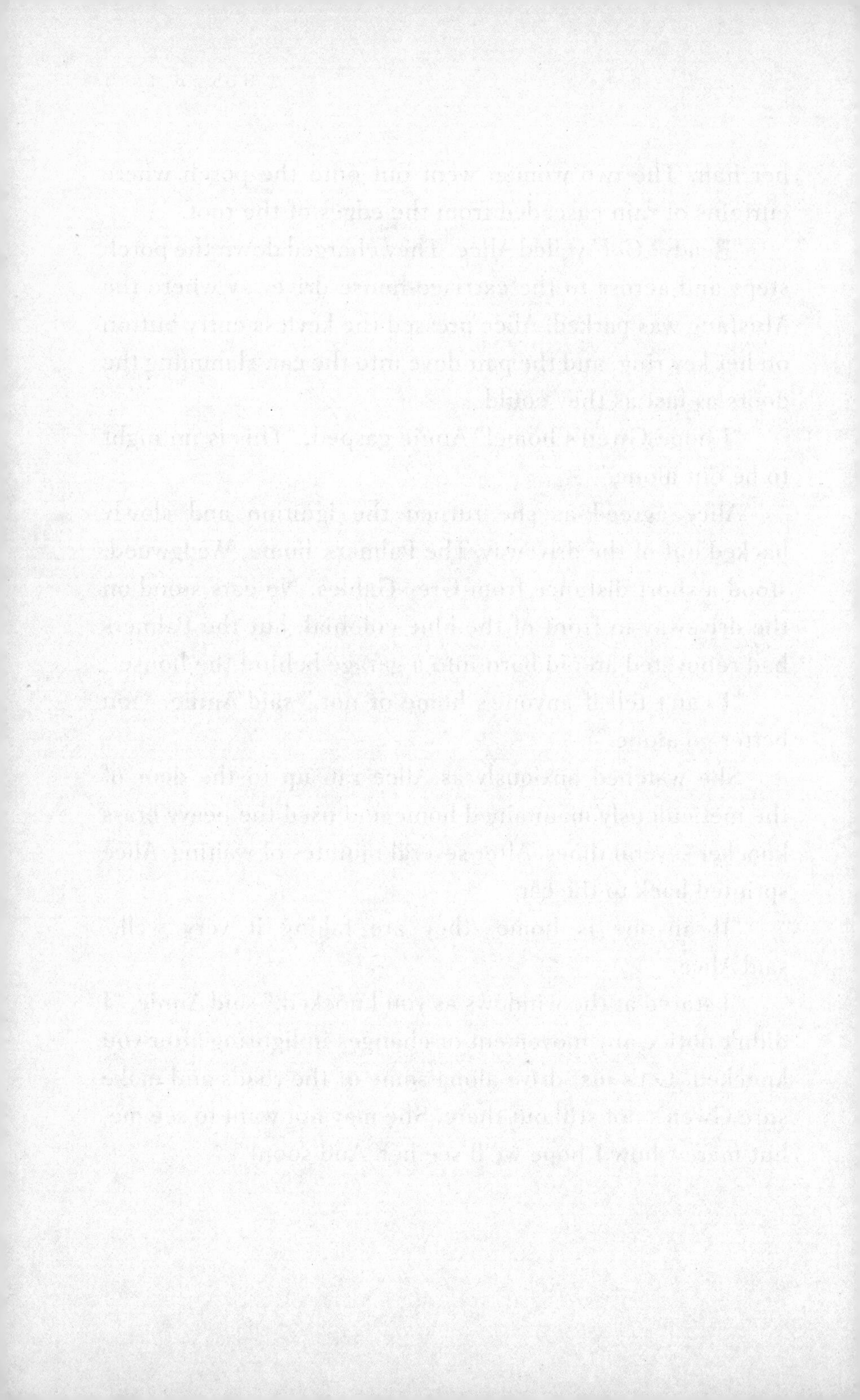

19

Annie and Alice decided to drive toward Main Street first, hoping Gwen had not strayed from hard-surface roads. Walking trails or paths could wash out from under one's feet in such a storm. Annie peered out her window. "It's like trying to see something behind a waterfall." Alice muttered, "Yup," putting all her energy into keeping the car on the right side of the road and stealing looks to the left beyond the roadside. They reached Main Street without seeing another human being.

"She wouldn't have kept going south on Main, would she?" asked Annie.

"Can't think of a reason why she would," answered Alice, idling the car at the corner of Maple and Main. "There's next to nothing there for miles."

"Let's take Oak to Ocean and then cover Grand. If we don't see Gwen on that route, I don't know where else she might be, other than home at Wedgwood."

"Do you suppose she might have turned to Reverend Wallace?" Alice kept an eye on the rearview mirror.

"I'd be relieved if she did. He is a wise, caring man. Hmmm, instead of Oak, maybe you should go down Elm past the church and manse." When at home, Reverend Wallace received visitors either in his home office or the parlor, both of which were located on the street side of the manse.

"If we see a light shining in one of the first-floor windows, there's a chance Gwen has found some help."

Alice turned right onto Main Street, crossed over Oak Lane, and turned right again onto Elm Street. The Town Square and ballpark stood empty and forlorn. Water sluiced over a large banner that advertised Harvest on the Harbor, causing it to sag between the two lampposts to which it was tied.

As the car approached the manse, Alice sighed. "Oh. The front rooms are dark, except on the second floor. Grand Avenue, here we come." Alice turned back onto Ocean Drive, past Grey Gables, and continued onto Grand Avenue. Of the three buildings located across from the Harbor, only The Grand Avenue Fish House showed any signs of life with lights winking through the storm.

The car had just passed the Snack Bar when Annie cried out, "Slow down, Alice! Do you see a person on your left or am I imagining things?" Alice braked carefully on the slick road from a crawl to barely moving.

Head bent and shoulders hunched, a slight figure fought against the elements. "I recognize that coat. It's Gwen's!" Alice lowered her window halfway down, ignoring the rain splashing into her face.

"Gwen!" she shouted as loudly as she could. "Let me give you a ride!" The figure stopped and turned to peer at the car. Gwen bent her head down again and continued picking her way along the road.

Annie tapped Alice on the shoulder. "Tell her John came to Grey Gables because he was so worried about her."

Alice nodded and turned back to the window. "Gwen!

John came by Grey Gables earlier. He's very worried about you." Gwen lifted a foot to step forward, and then lowered it to the same spot it had been and stood still. Alice put on her emergency blinkers and emergency brake before jumping out of the car to open the way to the backseat. Keeping her eyes trained on the ground, Gwen jogged across the street and slid into the rear seat.

Alice turned off the blinking emergency lights and drove a short distance farther along Grand Avenue to turn around at the Ocean View Assisted Living entrance.

"Gwen, you must be freezing!" Annie cried over the pounding of the rain and the slapping of the windshield wipers. "Can we take you to Grey Gables and get some dry clothes for you?"

Although she did not answer vocally, Gwen lifted her head enough to show agreement.

"I don't know about you, but I could go for some hot cocoa," Alice said, relief smoothing the lines of worry that had been stretched across her forehead. They passed the harbor again, the beacon from Butler Lighthouse appearing brighter than a few minutes before.

"Hot cocoa, tea, coffee, whatever's your pleasure." Annie tried to keep a balance between false heartiness and stifling concern to make the ride as comfortable as possible for Gwen. Annie had let her attention drift to the sound of the rain when Gwen said quietly, "Thank you, Alice, Annie." After John's words to her, the last thing Annie expected to hear from Gwen was gratitude. Although she still did not know the source of Gwen's pain, the core of tension that had been tightening stopped, and began to unwind.

Alice pulled into the driveway of Grey Gables. Glancing at the dashboard clock, Annie saw they had only been gone for thirty minutes.

When they bustled through the door, Boots sat right inside but retreated to the stairs in disgust as water drops flicked from hats and coats. Even the expensive raincoat Gwen wore could not stand up to the Maine storm. Every inch of her clothing ranked somewhere on the moisture spectrum from damp to sopping wet.

"Alice, will you take our coats to the mudroom while I find some warm clothes for Gwen?" Annie asked.

"Sure." Alice gathered the dripping coats, holding them at arm's length to give them a quick shake over the entry rug before carrying them as fast as she could to deposit them on the row of hooks attached to the wall.

"Come up with me, Gwen. If you'd like to take a warm shower, I have a comfy robe you can use. Gram always made sure she had extras."

Gwen's usually sleek blond hair was plastered against her head, the tidy chignon barely hung on, listing sideways with stray wet tendrils crawling down her neck. Gwen fingered the mess. "That sounds heavenly, Annie."

She walked over to the rug, took off her shoes, and arranged them neatly in the corner. Then she followed Annie up the stairs, Boots springing up ahead of them. Annie paused at the linen closet in the hallway long enough to grab fresh towels and escorted Gwen to the bath at the end of the hall. Placing the towels in Gwen's hands, Annie told her, "I'll hang some clothes on the doorknob for you. We'll be down in the kitchen."

"May I use your phone?" Gwen asked. "I need to let John know I'm all right."

"Of course!" Annie exclaimed. "I know he's worried about you. Let me get you the cordless from my bedroom."

Gwen murmured her thanks and continued into the spacious bath, while Annie turned into the master bedroom to get the telephone and to find clothes suited for her friend.

When Gwen entered the kitchen thirty-five minutes later in soft celery green pants and a long-sleeve tunic, her blond hair was dry and draping over her shoulders. Her shivers had fled under the soothing warm shower. Annie looked up from spooning cocoa powder and sugar into three mugs.

"Gwen! I've never seen you with your hair down before. How beautiful!"

Alice sat at the kitchen table with a basket of scones in front of her, which she had retrieved from the carriage house while Gwen had been upstairs. "Now that I think of it, neither have I. I never realized how wonderfully thick it is." She patted the chair next to her.

Gwen pulled out the chair and sat. "Oh, thank you. I don't think about my hair much."

"Is there any particular reason you always wear it up?" asked Alice.

Gwen opened her mouth to answer but closed it again to consider her answer. Light laughter escaped her. "I think it started from watching old Grace Kelly movies. She was so elegant. I grew up wanting to be like her."

Annie drizzled a little milk into each mug and stirred until a thick chocolate syrup gleamed. "Personally, I'd say you've mastered elegant very well."

Gwen's eyes turned somber and she lowered them, staring at her hands which rested in her lap. "I tossed elegant right out of the window this week, I'm afraid. In the process John has been hurt, as well as you, Annie. I'm so sorry."

Gwen paused.

"Thanks for letting me call John," she said. "I told him I'm with Alice. I was afraid he was still mad at you, Annie. I said I was going to shower and get warm, and that then I would come home. He was so relieved! Hopefully his anger will be relieved, too, when we have a chance to talk about all of this calmly."

Annie turned off the flame under the saucepan of milk, and poured the hot milk into each mug. "Gwen, please don't worry about me. We Texas gals are tough. I only wanted to support you in whatever you were experiencing, and I guess I stumbled over myself doing it." Annie set a mug in front of Gwen and then Alice. She took the third mug from the counter and sat down next to Gwen.

Gwen slowly stirred her hot chocolate. "The only thing you stumbled over, Annie, was a family secret. So secret I knew nothing about it." She lifted the mug and breathed in the scent of chocolate. Then she looked at her two friends. "Clara Stewart is my great-grandmother."

"And Evelyn Stewart?" asked Annie. "She was in the registry too, but there was no married name given."

Gwen nodded. "Yes, she is my grandmother, Evelyn Stewart Campbell. She sounds so Scottish, doesn't she? I had absolutely no idea there was any Passamaquoddy blood in my family line. Grandma and Mother never said a word."

"No wonder you turned so pale when I told you about Annie and me finding the end of the poem!" said Alice. "And here I thought you had probably been hit with insomnia the night before your trip to the museum."

"The insomnia didn't hit until after our conversation," Gwen said wryly. "I went home and tore through Wedgwood, looking at any paper, journal, or letter from my family for any mention of Passamaquoddy heritage. Dinner burned to a crisp. I couldn't tell John yet; I didn't know what to say. It wasn't the welcome home from work John was expecting." She took a sip of her cocoa. "Mmm—Alice, cocoa was a great choice."

"It's hard to go wrong with chocolate." Alice lifted the cloth from the basket in front of her. "Would you like a scone to go with it? I made them to test Annie's first batch of rose-hip jelly."

Gwen nodded. "I've eaten little in the last couple of days. One of your scones is a good way to get back into the habit of eating." She reached into the basket to take a scone and placed it on one of the dessert plates stacked next to the basket. Breaking off a tip of the treat, she nibbled off a small bite.

After swallowing she continued. "I don't want you to misunderstand about John from what I said. When he came home to a ruined dinner, he wasn't disturbed that his dinner wasn't perfect. He's never seen me like I've been the last few days. That's the first time I've burned a meal in thirty-five years of marriage!"

"That's quite a record," said Alice. "I think I burned the first five dinners I made in my marriage. It took years of practice to become the culinary genius I am today." Alice lifted her scone, its top now shimmering with the bright rose-hip jelly. "Did you ever find anything in your family's records?" She slid the jelly jar over to Gwen, who dabbed some on her own scone as she answered.

"No. And the more I looked, the more frustrated I became and the more worried John became. When I finally tried to explain what had happened, I became even more upset, realizing that my grandmother and mother had completely jettisoned an entire section of our family. And I wondered how it would impact my life." Gwen turned to Annie. "John thought I was angry because you had shared Grandma's name with Alice. But I wasn't. First, I was angry at my mother and grandmother for hiding my past from me. Second, it irked me that John went into his Mr. Fix-It mode." Gwen paused for another sip of cocoa as her friends inwardly smiled at her description of John's reaction. "I realize John's problem-solving skills have kept Stony Point Savings Bank strong in all kinds of economic ups and downs over the years, but I'm his wife, not a financial institution."

At that moment, Annie and Alice both knew their friend would weather her emotional storm. Annie nodded agreement. "That explains John's visit earlier. He thought I had hurt you, and the thought that I might have hurt you horrified me."

"What I don't understand," said Alice "is why the box, collar, and poem ended up in Betsy's attic. If your grandmother and mother didn't want you to know about that part of your heritage, why not sell or throw away the things?" She stirred the remaining cocoa in her mug before draining it.

"That's just one of the many questions I've been asking myself," said Gwen. "I don't know if Mother even knew. She just kept telling me to 'marry well' and 'do unto others.' Maybe Grandma kept the information from her too."

"It seems to me that whoever left the things at Grey Gables didn't want to permanently close the door to that heritage," said Annie. "Since the door has been opened, Gwen, would you like to take your heirlooms home? The zippered tote I had kept them in is waterproofed so they should be safe from the rain."

"I would appreciate seeing them again," Gwen answered. "But would you mind keeping them here for a while? At least until things have calmed down some at home, and I've begun to figure out who I am."

Annie stood. "I'd be happy to keep them for you. I'll be right back." She walked down the hall to the living room, where the zippered bag sat next to her crochet bag. Boots had reclaimed the couch now that the house was quiet again. Back in the kitchen Annie placed the bag on the empty chair on the other side of Gwen.

Gwen popped the last bite of scone into her mouth. "Annie, you must have used Betsy's jelly recipe. Every bite reminds me of her."

Annie smiled. "Yes, I did. Since this first batch appears to be a success, I'll be making more. Now we just have to convince Alice to keep the scones coming."

"I seem to remember the jelly being very tasty on toast too," replied Alice, laughing. "But I don't have any plans to stop baking any time soon."

Gwen went to the sink to rinse the crumbs from her

hands and thoroughly dry them. She unzipped the tote and took out the box. She held it in her hands for a moment. "So light," she marveled, "yet it holds the voice of a family line I never knew existed."

Annie remembered her emotions when she had thought the items might have had their origins in her own family and the sense of betrayal with which she had wrestled.

Gwen took off the lid and drew out the regalia collar, staring at it as though memorizing the exact position of each tiny bead. Just as Annie had done the day she had found it in the attic, she held it around her neck.

"It's beautiful with your coloring," Alice said.

"To think this touched my great-grandmothers neck, and maybe Grandmother's too." Gwen's voice trailed off, and she sat silently looking at the only heirlooms she had of her family from Sipayik.

"Gwen, I have a printout of the Mitchell family line, Clara's family," said Annie. "It goes back to the American Revolution and indicates one of your family members was a captain. It might have fallen to the bottom of the tote."

Gwen reached into the tote and pulled out the pages. Her eyes bright, she murmured, "Oh, Annie. This is overwhelming, but thank you!" She looked up to include Alice. "Thank you both for coming to find me on a night like tonight."

"And don't forget, we made you cocoa." Alice smiled.

"What more can a woman ask of her friends?" said Gwen. She glanced at the clock on the stove. "I should be getting back to Wedgwood. I can't imagine what John is thinking by now."

Alice stood. "Your carriage awaits, m'lady." She went to the mudroom to retrieve their coats. "They're a little less soaking wet."

Gwen went to Annie. Hugging her, she whispered. "You are a Holden, through and through. Don't let anyone tell you that's anything less than incredible." She shrugged her coat over her shoulders and buttoned it high.

Annie escorted her two friends to the door and watched as they dashed to the Mustang. She whispered softly, "Lord, you knew what you were doing!"

20

Morning found the rain gone, a blanket of fog in its place. Annie stood at her bedroom window, peering out to determine its thickness. Boots was stretched out on the bed, as if still recuperating from the previous evening's excitement.

"Definitely not the pea-soup variety of fog," Annie informed the cat. "I can still see some of the roses a little down the hill. Todd would probably call it light fog." She wanted to visit Cecil but decided to wait until afternoon, keeping an eye on the fog. There was more work to be done in the library and more crochet than she could shake a hook at. There was plenty to fill the morning. After spending so many hours in the car the day before, Annie looked forward to doing something more active, so when she had finished breakfast she headed for the library.

Eyeballing Grandpa's journals, she estimated she would need to buy six more storage boxes from Malone's. A thick book stuck out at an awkward angle from the shelf above the journals. Annie reached out to realign it. Another cookbook. The title on the spine read *Bountiful Harvest Cookbook*. "Hey, this might have the perfect recipes for Thanksgiving," Annie murmured. She pulled the book from the shelf to move it to the baker's rack in the kitchen where the other cookbooks were stored. Flipping through the book, she checked out some of the recipes. The book flopped open at one point, where a small envelope was wedged between two pages. Thinking it was another fan letter for Gram, Annie withdrew the note from the envelope and read:

December 10, 1941

Dear Betsy,

Please keep these safe. Wedding soon and Grandfather kicked out of House.

E.S.

"E.S.!" Annie gasped. "Could it be?" She put the book on the baker's rack shelf with the other cookbooks and read the short note again.

"1941.That's before Gram had even met Grandpa. Gram was only … nineteen." She remembered Alice calling Gram "a safe place." Evidently, she had been one from her youth. Annie put the note in a pocket of her jeans and hoped she could find a way to get it to Gwen without John knowing. He needed some time to decompress after his visit.

Annie made herself return to the library. What she really wanted to do was to take every book from every shelf, shake them, and read every single thing that fluttered to the floor.

"Stay focused!" she chided herself. "You're supposed to be preparing for LeeAnn's visit, not investigating." At the end of two hours Annie looked at the results of her efforts, pleased. She hardly recognized the room compared to the state it had been in when she had first returned to Stony Point. The wood floor was lovely, now that she could see more of it.

After all the bending and reaching, Annie was ready to sit for a while. Retreating to the living room, Annie picked up the crochet she had dropped the night before when John had banged on the door. She worked to the sound of moisture dripping from the porch rails, a gentler sound than the night's torrents. When she finished the second piece of the pillow, she carried both rounds to the kitchen to soak them in cool water. After shaping them, Annie left the pieces to dry on the counter.

On her way out of the kitchen, Annie took a jar of jelly from the shelf for Cecil. Over the course of the morning, the fog had lightened a little, and Annie was comfortable driving in it for the short ride down Grand Avenue. After she entered Ocean View Assisted Living through the main entrance, she hung her coat by the entry and headed first for the large common room. If Cecil couldn't be out near the water, she thought he might be in the room with the giant window overlooking it. Annie paused at the edge of the room to scan the area for her friend.

Make it two friends. A grin broke out on her face as she heard Gwen's voice call out, "Annie! Over here!" Cecil and Gwen sat together in one of the conversation nooks in front of the window. She hurried over, dropping into the cozy chair next to Cecil. Annie was happy to see that the hurt and confusion had left Gwen's eyes.

"Have I missed all the fun?" she asked.

Cecil looked tired to her, but he smiled and said, "There's plenty of time for more."

"Cecil has been telling me some of the history of the Passamaquoddy people," said Gwen. "He was just going to tell me some of the creation stories and Glooskap when I saw you."

"Oh, good. I got here at the right time, then." Annie leaned forward, propping her chin in her hand. "Which one first?"

"In honor of the birch-bark box that we now know belongs to Gwen, I thought I'd start with Glooskap and the Birch Tree." Cecil looked at the two women who nodded their heads like children being asked if they'd like some ice cream.

"When Glooskap was naming the birch tree, it is said that he asked it to take care of our people. But one time he found a straight birch tree and wanted to make it into a canoe. When Glooskap cut the tree down, it almost killed him. The narrow escape angered him. He also had a very difficult time freeing himself from its branches, angering him even more. Enraged, Glooskap grabbed a stick and beat the birch as hard as he could from the tip to the roots. He ordered the gashes he had made to stay forever as eyes so that never again would anyone be killed—or almost killed by—a birch."

"They do look like slitty eyes!" Annie laughed.

"Would that the eyes on my birch-bark box could tell me everything they have seen," said Gwen. "I still know nothing about how it ended up at Grey Gables."

"Oh!" Annie clapped a hand over her jeans pocket. "I found something in my library that might help shed a little more light—and probably spark more questions too, I'm afraid." She pulled out the note and handed it to Gwen.

Gwen's eyes widened as she read the short note. "Didn't Charley and Betsy buy Grey Gables after they married? It didn't belong to either of their families, right? This seems to indicate Grandmother left the box with her in 1941!"

"No, Grey Gables wasn't in the family. Grandpa was originally from Connecticut. Gram's family lived right in town. I think that's where your grandmother must have originally taken the box. Do you have any idea what it means about her grandfather being kicked out of the house? And was the wedding hers or someone else's? The Tribe registry said Evelyn was born in 1906, so she would have been 35."

Gwen thought for a moment. "Grandmother married a second time after her first husband was killed while working at a lime quarry. Campbell was her second husband's name. Grandpop Campbell wasn't officially my grandfather, but he was the only one I knew. Mother's father was Joseph Hobbs. Why would her grandfather be kicked out of the house?"

"The note is dated 1941? May I see it?" asked Cecil. Gwen handed him the note. Cecil nodded when he reached the last part of the sentence. "As I suspected. Did you notice how Evelyn capitalized the word 'house'? I believe she was not referring to a family home but Maine's House of Representatives. Tension had been building for years, arguments over the role and rights of the Passamaquoddy and Penobscot representatives. General anti-Indian feelings continued to grow until 1941 when the tribal representatives were kicked out of their seats."

"How horrible," said Gwen. "I remember Grandmother being very concerned with what people thought about her and the family." A faint ironic smile came to her lips. "Occasionally she would chide me if she didn't think I was dressed appropriately, which usually meant I had forgotten my gloves. If her grandfather had been kicked out of a government seat, it surely made the newspapers." Gwen sighed. "Yes, I guess I can see how she might have thought she was making things easier for her children by hiding part of her heritage."

"I'm grieved that she thought she needed to," said Annie somberly. "From the research I did after I first found the box, I think many people of American Indian ancestry ended up doing the same thing because of economic or safety concerns."

"It was difficult to be a Passamaquoddy in the 1940s," said Cecil. "Even though many served in the American Armed Forces during both World Wars, there was much distrust. The living conditions were unhealthy and didn't improve significantly until after 1980, and not without much struggle and sacrifice. As much as I loved my people at Sipayik, living there was very hard. Your grandmother had before her two painful paths from which to choose."

"Yes, she did." Gwen reached over and placed a hand over Cecil's, which rested near his knee. "Thank you, Cecil. You've been so helpful."

"Come whenever you want to learn more," said Cecil. "You can't be Passamaquoddy and only know one Glooskap story."

Gwen laughed. "I will visit again after my next volunteer shift. Right now I need to go get dinner started. John has calmed down since last night, but I'm sure he would appreciate a return to home-cooked dinners, especially ones that aren't burnt."

"I'll walk you to the door," said Annie. "I brought something for Cecil, and I left it in my coat pocket." The two women walked toward the entrance.

"Annie, I meant what I said about John. He's doing much better, since I'm beginning to process everything. Just knowing my maternal ancestry includes another Revolutionary War veteran, in its own way, was helpful for us both. I'm thankful that you drove all the way to Sipayik to bring the information back on what turned out to be my family line. I'm also glad that you cleaned in your library this morning and found the letter. Between you and Cecil, I'm starting to understand why my grandmother would do what she did. Peace is returning—and it's a deeper peace."

"I think Harvest on the Harbor this year is going to be quite a celebration," said Annie. "I can't wait to see your knitting." They reached the coat racks, and Annie pulled the jelly jar from the pocket of her coat.

"I was struggling with what to design, but I'm finding inspiration from Grandmother's regalia collar. And that's all I'm going to say."

"It will be gorgeous. Expert handwork runs in your family." Annie smiled.

"As it does in yours." Gwen smiled back. "Bye, Annie."

Annie walked back to the common room. Cecil's eyes were closed, and he was breathing deeply. Not wanting to disturb him, Annie left the jelly with the resident concierge attendant to be delivered to Cecil when he awoke.

As Annie drove past the harbor she realized the fog was gone.

21

The next month whirled along for the residents of Stony Point in a flurry of activities. Fishermen brought the ocean's bounty for cauldron-size pots of chowder. The ladies held a chowder cook-off to decide whose recipe would be used on the big day. Todd Butler and his crew strung the lobster shacks with orange and white lights. Fathers worked alongside their teenagers, demonstrating how to build sturdy booths. Doc Witham and Chessey Cushman sharpened their knives to expertly carve pumpkins. Gardeners nurtured pots of flowers until they exploded with autumn colors. The members of the Hook and Needle Club cross-stitched, knitted, quilted, and crocheted until their fingers were numb.

The day of Harvest on the Harbor arrived. Mary Beth had instructed the club members to bring their handcrafts an hour and a half before the festival's opening to the booth manned by A Stitch In Time. She, of course, had come even earlier and had unpacked a variety of fabric remnants, boxes, and table stands for displaying every piece to catch the shopper's eye and wallet. Peggy was the first to drop off her quilt before hurrying to help set up and serve at The Cup & Saucer booth.

"Gotta hurry, Mary Beth," she said, thrusting a large bag into Mary Beth's hands. Her fingernails were painted dark green with bright orange pumpkins in the middle of each nail. "I hope you can get a decent amount for it."

Mary Beth drew the red and yellow quilt from the bag. "Peggy! Are you kidding me? I wish you'd had time to make five more. We could have sold all of them easily."

"You're a *love*, Mary Beth." Relief rang in every syllable. "Take a break sometime and come by our booth, OK?"

Mary Beth leaned over the table and hollered after Peggy as she hurried to help her boss. "I am *not* a love, either! I'm a good businesswoman!" Then, she shook her head with a smile and got back to work, draping the quilt with that secret technique she had until the cattails on the quilt looked like they were gently swaying in a breeze.

Alice and Annie walked together to the harbor, Alice sipping the coffee Annie had brought to her door in a travel mug. "The coffee is so good, I can almost forgive you for calling me at such a disgusting hour," said Alice, stifling a yawn.

"Hey, Mary Beth set the time for us to bring our projects, and the committee set the start time for Harvest on the Harbor," Annie reminded her. "I'm just an innocent bystander."

"Hmph! Need to have a discussion with the mayor about this."

"You can give it a try," Annie said as they approached the docks. "But remember, Ian still keeps military hours. I'm not sure he'll understand your pain." She lifted the big bag she was carrying that bulged with pillows. "Personally, I'm glad we had to come early before the crowds. I'd be knocking people into the water with this."

"Easy for you to say, Little Miss Sunrise." Alice tilted her head back to retrieve the last precious drops of her coffee.

Annie nudged her friend's arm. "There's Mary Beth. Look at Peggy's quilt! That's not going to last long."

Mary Beth saw them coming. "Ah! More merchandise. Let me see what you've got."

"A pillow fight's worth of pillows, that's what I've got," Annie said, laughing.

"Well, hand 'em over so I can get them arranged. The opening will be here before we know it." Mary Beth walked around the booth to take the bulky bag from Annie. "Thank you both for volunteering to help today. I think it's going to be our busiest year yet, and Kate will only be here part of the time. Vanessa's volleyball team is sponsoring a booth, and all the parents have to take a time slot." Mary Beth pulled out a pillow and then another, holding them out to get a good look. "Annie, these are wonderful. The colors are neutral enough to fit almost every decor and the sea-urchin shape and the stripes give it both a whimsical *and* sophisticated feel. That's not easy to do, you know."

"The hardest part was getting them stuffed and sewn together right!" Annie laughed. "But I really enjoyed using the Tunisian technique again."

"And the shoppers will enjoy buying your pillows today, no doubt about it," Alice said, starting to look perkier now that some caffeine was in her system. She set her bag on the table. "Here are my Micmac-inspired place mats."

The three woman were bent over Alice's cross-stitched mats when they heard Jason's New York accent. "Good morning, ladies."

"Good morning, Jason," they chorused. Alice mugged in her best gangster impression, "Do you have the goods?" They all knew Stella was helping at the booth run by the Cultural Center all day.

Jason grinned and lifted a wide briefcase, setting it on the table next to the placemats. With a touch he sprang the lock and raised the top. All three of the crafters caught their breath in delight. Mary Beth drew out one of the scarves, the color of an icy blue river with currents and islands depicted in beige. "Fine, fine work, as always," Mary Beth murmured.

"Oh, is that Stella's project?" Gwen's voice startled them. "I hope I can reach her level of perfection some day!" She reached out to lightly finger the edge of the scarf. "It's one hundred percent wool too. It will be so cozy and warm in the cold."

"Gwen, I've seen some pretty perfect work from you too," said Mary Beth. "You have something for us, right?"

Kate hurried up to the booth before Gwen could answer. "Hi, everyone! Sorry I'm a little late. I needed to drop Vanessa off at the volleyball booth, and one of the coaches started asking me about the display. Guess he figured I'd been trained by the best and wanted to make good use of my training." She scanned the pieces that were already on the table. "Oh, Stella was so right about this theme. The shoppers are going to love the variety!"

"Gwen was just going to show us her pieces," said Annie.

"Well, what are you waiting for?" Kate laughed. "I'm dying to see too."

Gwen opened her tote bag and drew out several knit evening purses with beading. Everyone recognized the pattern of delicate green leaves with lavender and periwinkle flowers from the regalia collar.

"I thought it would be appropriate to use a design from Great-Grandmother's collar," Gwen said. "It's funny, isn't it? A part of my heritage was just like that beautifully beaded piece—boxed in, locked up, and hidden away. Annie freed both with her discovery and her curiosity. For that, I am blessed, and I am thankful."

Silence fell over the little group as each friend thought of the journey the pattern had traveled to end up in the exquisite purses. Eyes misted over like a foggy morning in Maine. Annie was the first to speak.

"Gwen, the purses are beautiful," she said, almost in a whisper, "but the beauty of you finding the pathway to your Passamaquoddy past … well, that's almost miraculous."

Jason coughed uneasily, feeling out of place in that private moment between the friends. "If you ladies will excuse me, I need to get back to Stella."

Mary Beth looked up. "Of course, Jason. Tell Stella we all love her scarves, and we're sure everyone else will too." Jason tipped his hat and strode away. "If I had known this was going to be so emotional, I think I would have had everyone bring their things yesterday." She turned to Kate. "OK, go ahead. Finish this amazing collection we've got going."

"Vanessa wanted to help too," said Kate. "She made coffee-cup cozies, using some of our leftover yarns." She opened her large tote bag and set several handfuls of cozies of different colors and thickness on the table.

"What a clever idea!" said Alice. She plucked up a thick silk cozy in a bright, multicolored yarn of purples, blues, reds, and greens. "I want this one." She reached into her pocket for her wallet.

"Be sure to tell Vanessa that she made the first sale," said Mary Beth. "That girl has a future at A Stitch In Time, just like her mother."

Kate smiled. "I will." She reached into the tote again and drew out one of her shawls. "I made them in a few different colors." She spread out a triangular shawl in dark red. They saw that she had taken the curator's advice and had chosen not to add any beading. The shawls didn't need them. The evergreen tree pattern had more than enough impact on its own. Not one to draw attention to herself, Kate quickly emptied her tote and stored it under the booth. "We better get these displayed," she said, looking at her watch. "It won't be long before folks start arriving."

"I need to go help John at the bank's display," said Gwen. She smiled at Annie and Alice. "We're serving hot cocoa and apple cider." She fingered the pile of cozies. "Would it be OK to bring some of these to our booth?"

Mary Beth nodded. "That's a great idea, Gwen. If you run out, just call me on my cell phone, and I'll have someone run more to you."

Gwen scooped up several cozies. "Bye, everyone!"

Mary Beth put Alice and Annie to work, and the display was finished before the first comers arrived. Ian came by on his tour of all the booths, making sure everyone had what they needed for a successful Harvest celebration. He admired the display of handcrafts. "The club has topped all prior years with their work this time, Mary Beth. I didn't know how you were going to do that!" His eyes rested on the blue and white urchin pillows. "Becky keeps telling me I need some 'accent pieces' in my house. These would look fine on my sofa, I think. I'll take two and be your first sale of the day."

"Too late, Mayor. I beat you to it." Alice crowed. "But your sister-in-law is right. Your house could do with a little more oomph." She reached under the booth's table for a bag.

"A person's got to get up mighty early to beat you, Alice," Ian faked a wince as he pulled out some neatly folded bills.

"Yes, that is definitely the only sure way," said Annie, laughing.

Ian paid for his pillows and continued on the final part of his inspection. It wasn't long before the four women were all helping customers and sharing the inspiration for the pieces. Annie was relieved when she saw Cecil shortly after the starting time. She'd wanted him to see as many of the handcrafts as possible before they were sold. A crowd of family surrounded him, most bearing a Lewey resemblance. After making introductions, Cecil turned to Mary Beth.

"Miss Brock, your club has honored the Passamaquoddy people with your expert and thoughtful art," Cecil said solemnly. "Thank you."

"Mr. Lewey, I think I can speak for all the members and say it has been a project of the heart more than we ever imagined it would be," Mary Beth replied.

"I feel like we're the ones that have had the honor to be able to do this and learn so much," said Alice. Kate and Annie nodded their agreement.

Martin, Cecil's son, pulled out his camera. "Do you mind if I take some photos of the pieces?" he asked.

"Only if you promise to send me some copies at the store," Mary Beth answered.

"I'd be glad to," Martin said, his camera already up to his eye. When he finished, the family moved along to enjoy the other displays and allow other people to see the handcrafted pieces.

Before noon arrived, the four ladies stood before an empty

display. Mary Beth stood with her hands on her hips, looking at the table. "I know I said the pieces would sell fast, but I didn't expect to be done by lunch!"

"That's a first," said Alice. "Now we can go enjoy the other displays. And I could really go for some of that chowder."

Annie rubbed her hands together. "And some of that hot cocoa to go with it."

"How about you go get us cocoa, and I'll snag the chowder. Then meet me back at the picnic tables," Alice suggested.

"You're on. Do y'all want to join us?" Annie asked Mary Beth and Kate.

"I might find you at the tables in a while," answered Mary Beth. "I want to get the rest of the table packed up so we don't confuse the afternoon crowd."

Kate shook her head. "I'd love to, but I'm due over at the volleyball booth soon. I'll have to grab something quick."

"We'll pop over to see you and Vanessa," said Alice. Then she and Annie left to find their food.

Annie realized as she was weaving through the crowd that she might be about to face John. She hadn't seen him all month. Her crochet and jelly-making had kept her at home most of the time. Gwen had told her John had adjusted to the changes in Gwen, but Annie didn't know if he'd changed his mind about "that meddler."

"If Gwen's ancestors could face all the challenges they had forced on them, surely I can face one bank president," Annie muttered. As she approached the bank's booth, she quickly prayed for grace. "Hi, Gwen. Hi, John," she said. "Alice and I have been dreaming of your hot cocoa all morning."

Gwen smiled at her. "How is business?"

"We sold out!" Annie exclaimed. "Your purses practically flew off the table."

"Oh, that's wonderful. The community pantry should be able to give away more turkey dinners than even last year."

John had been staring at the urn of cider but lifted his eyes to look at Annie. "The Hook and Needle Club has accomplished a great service to the community."

"Thank you, John," said Annie. "I think we have all gained much more than we gave."

After a moment of silence, John spoke again, "Annie, would you take a quick walk with me?" Gwen smiled encouragement to her.

"Sure," Annie said. John left the booth, and they walked slowly away from the line of booths.

"I want to apologize for my behavior last month," John began. "There is no excuse for my hasty reaction." He paused. "I hope you can forgive me."

"John, I already have," said Annie. "You were worried about Gwen, and I know how that feels."

"I shouldn't have lost control. I said things that weren't true."

"As someone who has spoken in haste more times than she can ever count, I can hardly hold that against you, John." Annie smiled up at him. "Would you and Gwen like to have some chowder with Alice and me?"

"I'll let Gwen speak for herself, but I'm sure I can delegate the booth activity so we can get away for a bite to eat." They walked back to the booth, where Gwen enthusiastically accepted Annie's invitation and poured four cups of cocoa.

John detoured toward the chowder booth for two more

bowls of soup, while Annie and Gwen carried the cocoa over to where Alice sat.

"Hi, Gwen. I would have bought you a bowl of chowder if I'd known you were coming," said Alice.

Gwen sat across from her. "John went to get us some."

Alice smiled as she blew on the thick chowder filling her spoon. "Good! It smells amazing." She cautiously sipped some. "The judges got it right. This tastes as delicious as it smells."

"I'm glad the chowder hasn't sold out as fast as our projects," said Annie, picking up her spoon. "I'm starving."

"This has been the best Harvest day we've had yet," said Gwen. "The weather is as good as it can be."

"Remember that year with all the wind?" said Alice. "When the volunteer fire department's booth blew over and fell into the water? It was frigid!"

"And Todd Butler rescued it with his boat, hauling it in like a lobster trap," Gwen added, laughing.

"I think every year since then Reverend Wallace has been spending extra hours praying about the weather," added Alice.

"What am I missing?" John said as he set a bowl of soup in front of Gwen and sat down with his own.

"Memories of Harvest days past," answered Annie. "I'm not sure if I should be happy or sad that I wasn't here for them."

"Told her about the year with the bit of wind, did you?" John kept a straight face but his eyes held laughter.

Annie noticed Cecil and his family weaving between the picnic tables with bowls and stood to wave at them. "Cecil! Over here!" When the family drew close to the table, she said, "John and Gwen, have you met Cecil's family?"

Gwen smiled. "I think I've seen them all at one time or another at Ocean View but never all together at once." She introduced Martin and Nataline to John, who shook their hands.

"Do you think you can all fit?" John asked, waving at the rest of the table.

"We're used to squeezing together during meals at holidays," Nataline grinned. "We've gotten pretty good at it." The family demonstrated by managing to arrange themselves on the remaining bench space.

"Cecil, thank you for telling me about the Picture Rocks in Machias," Gwen said. "John is taking a day off next week, and we're going to go see them."

Cecil nodded. "I think you will find it a powerful experience, seeing petroglyphs made by Passamaquoddy people thousands of years ago."

"We're thinking of taking our children when they visit next time," said John. He turned to Gwen. "Did you tell Cecil about Maddy?"

"No, I haven't had a chance yet," replied Gwen. "Do you remember how Annie posted requests for information on some of the genealogy websites?"

Cecil nodded.

"Maddy replied to one of them. She's a relative of mine that I didn't know I had! We're going to meet at the Rocks and spend some time together."

Annie looked down the table filled with people eating, talking, and laughing. Her excitement over her family's visit for Thanksgiving had not waned at all. But now, more than ever, she knew that once the visit was over, she still had family in Stony Point.

About The Author

Karen Kelly has been gripped by a love of story as long as she can remember. After writing special features for a New York Times regional publication she turned to her first love, fiction for children and adults. Boxed In is her eighth published book. Karen lives in Florida, where she homeschools her three sons and enjoys off-road cycling, singing, exploring and taking classes at a classical study center. Over the years she has pursued a variety of handcrafts, such as cross-stitch, quilling, ceramics, and basket weaving. She looks forward to returning to them in the future.

ANNIE'S ATTIC MYSTERIES™

Join Annie Dawson and the members of the Hook and Needle Club of Stony Point, Maine, as they track down mysteries connected with the contents found in the attic of Annie's ancestral home, Grey Gables. There will be danger, adventures and heartwarming discoveries in the secrets Annie unearths—secrets about her own family as well as the townspeople of this charming seacoast town in central Maine. Let the good people of Stony Point warm your heart and the mysteries of Annie's Attic keep you on the edge of your seat.

To find out how to get other books in this series visit
AnniesMysteries.com